VOYAGE TO VICTORY

KIERAN FANNING

CODE 2 CRACKERS

This puzzle book belongs to

WITHDRAWN FROM STOCK
_____

MENTOR BOOKS

For the Brunner Boys

First Published 2001
by
MENTOR BOOKS
43 Furze Road,
Sandyford Industrial Estate,
Dublin 18.
Tel. +353 1 295 2112/3   Fax. +353 1 295 2114
e-mail: admin@mentorbooks.ie
www.mentorbooks.ie

ISBN: 1-84210-085-8

Copyright © 2001 Kieran Fanning

The right of Kieran Fanning to be identified as the
Author of the work has been asserted by him
in accordance with the Copyright Acts.

All rights reserved. No part of this publication may be
reproduced, stored in a retrieval system, or transmitted in
any form or by any means electronic, mechanical,
photocopying, recording, or otherwise,
without prior written permission of the publisher.

The Author
Originally from Stratford-on-Slaney,
Co. Wicklow, Kieran Fanning now lives in Co. Meath
and works as a primary school teacher in Dublin.

Illustrations by Kieran Fanning
Design and layout by Kathryn McKinney
Cover by Jon Berkeley
www.jonberkeley.com

Printed in Ireland by ColourBooks
1 3 5 7 9 10 8 6 4 2

Important Notice – Please read carefully!

This is not an ordinary book. You do not read straight through from beginning to end. Sam and Lisa need your help to solve puzzles and problems that occur in the story. The answer to a problem will be the next page of the story to turn to. Sometimes you will have to turn to a **page number** but sometimes you will have to follow a **symbol**. These are the little pictures at the top left-hand corner of every left-hand page. All symbols and their page numbers are listed below.

You must solve the puzzles and problems correctly to find out the next page to turn to. If you are correct you will see the answer in bold print at the top of the page. If you are wrong you should go back and try again. If you get really stuck on any problem there is an answers page at the back of the book.

It might help to write down the page you are working on each time, so if you get the answer wrong you can go back and try again.

Good Luck!

... **symbols**

... **page numbers**

VOYAGE TO VICTORY
2

The old bus chugged towards the Heritage Museum. Only five minutes to go. It was school tour time again and amid the shouting, paper flicking, singing and general chaos that existed on the bus sat two best friends, Sam and Lisa. Of course they were sitting away from each other because teachers never allow friends to sit together.

'You'll only get each other into trouble,' explained Miss Fussy.

It would, however, take more than Miss Fussy to keep Sam and Lisa apart because when these two friends got together, they could turn anything into an adventure, even a boring school tour.

The bus pulled over to the side of the road and stopped. Mr Groggy, the bus driver, leaned back in his seat and sighed. He unfolded a crumpled map and scratched his head in puzzlement.

Miss Fussy approached the front of the bus to assist.

'Here's where we are,' she said pointing to the map. 'Continue northwards, take the first right, then the second right, then left, then right, then left. The next place you come to will be the Heritage Museum.'

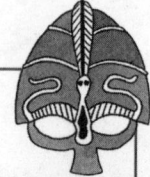

**Which number is the Heritage Museum?
Turn to the same page as your answer.**

VOYAGE TO VICTORY

3

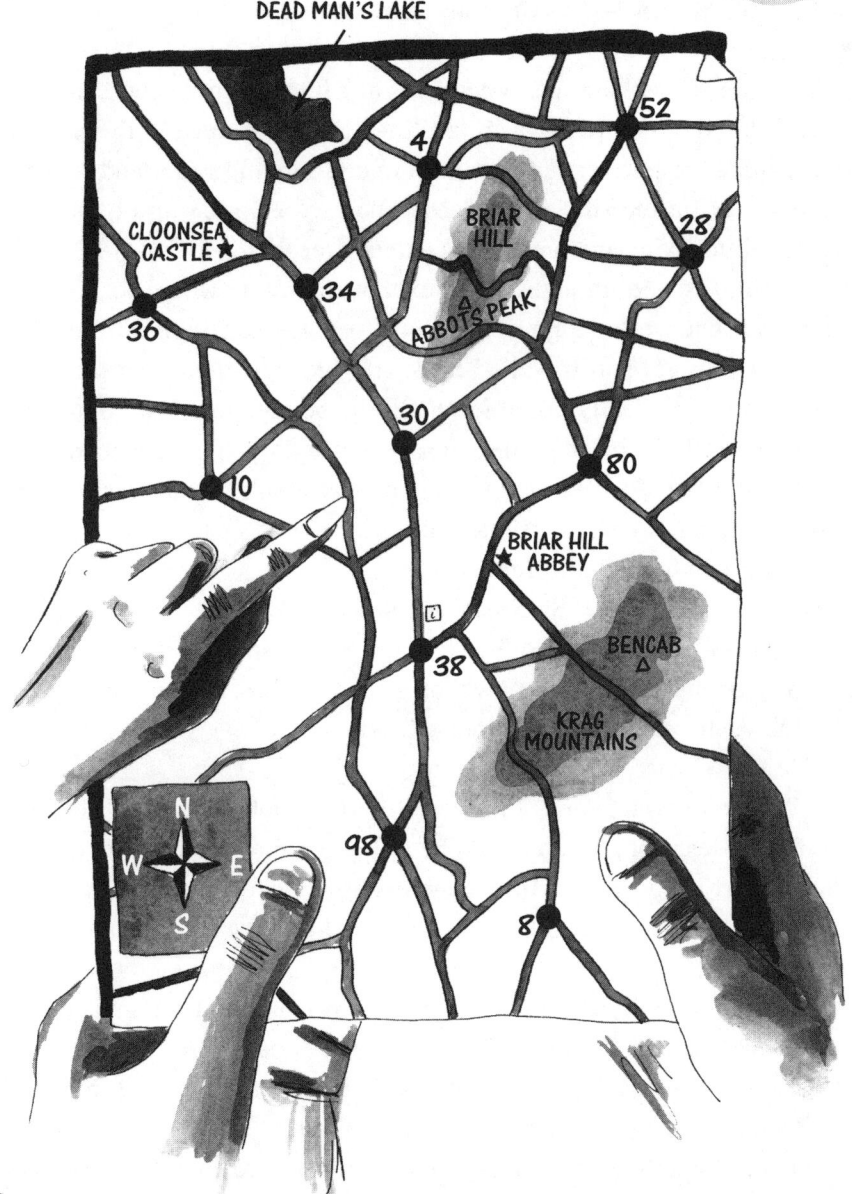

VOYAGE TO VICTORY

4

The flower symbol is the correct answer.

Sam woke up with a start. Where was he? It took him a few seconds to remember. He sat up. It was night-time. Stars glistened in the sky like fairy lights. Silence except for the sound of lapping water and snoring. Everybody on the ship was asleep. They were curled up on the deck with animal skins and woollen blankets over them.

I could escape, thought Sam, except there's nowhere to go! Is it possible that we have gone back in time? He had seen all the films where explorers had travelled back and indeed forwards in time but surely it wasn't really possible. Would he be able to return to his own time or would he be stuck here forever? Why had this happened? Was it something to do with the museum or that monk or that stupid book? His thoughts were interrupted by movement beside him. It was Brendan. He looked miserable.

'What year is this?' Sam asked him.

Brendan frowned. He looked at Sam with suspicion.

'You mean, you don't know?' he said. 'It's 828, of course!'

'Oh yeah,' said Sam. 'Of course it is!'

He knew what was coming next.

'Where are you from?' enquired Brendan, looking at Sam's boots.

The easiest thing to do would be to lie, but how would Sam explain his modern clothes and hair cut and his obvious ignorance about life in the year 828? He wished Lisa was awake. She'd be much better at this sort of thing.

'I'm from the future,' ventured Sam. 'At least I think I am.'

'Wow!' gasped Brendan. 'How did you get here?'

'I don't know,' began Sam. 'We were in this museum and then . . .'

Brendan interrupted him, 'What's a museum?'

Oh no! thought Sam. This is too hard. I've got to change the subject.

'Do you want your cross and beads back?' he asked Brendan. 'I can see who has them . . . and he's fast asleep!'

VOYAGE TO VICTORY

5

Who stole Brendan's cross and rosary beads?
If you can't remember, read page 104 again.
Turn to the same page as your answer.

Number six, Loki, is the correct god.

'Clever little mortals!' mused the god, pointing to one of the doors. 'You should find Odin in here and I'm sure you will be amazed by what you see.'

He smiled at the children as they passed by him. Lisa eyed him suspiciously. When they passed through the door, it banged behind them. They were shocked to hear a cackle of laughter from the other side, but even more shocked at the sight in front of them. An enormous room full of towering stone walls spread out in front of them. Sam, Lisa and Brendan were standing at the edge of a gigantic maze!

'You'll be *a-mazed* by what you see!' mimicked Sam. 'These gods are really funny guys!'

Lisa tried the door behind her. She wasn't surprised to find it locked.

'Well, looks like there's only one way to go,' said Brendan, entering the maze.

'To infinity and beyond!' shouted Sam, thrusting a fist into the air.

To which door does the maze lead the children?
Turn to the same page as your answer.

VOYAGE TO VICTORY
7

Eight cows is the correct answer.

'Right,' said Olaf when the children returned. 'I'll send someone to look for the strays.'

He began crossing the fields in long strides. The children scurried after him. The further they walked, the wetter the ground became. As they squelched through the bog, Olaf pointed out some of the other slaves carrying lumps of the bog in large pots.

'They're collecting bog ore,' he explained, 'to be melted down into iron. My son, the blacksmith, will then use this iron to make equipment – nails, weapons, helmets, shields and many other things.'

Soon they arrived at the corner of the field where two men were filling smelting furnaces with charcoal and bog ore. The furnaces were shaped like beehives. Black smoke billowed from the top of each one.

'Now that you've had the tour,' said Olaf to the children, 'you can go down to Olafsson's workshop and see if he needs any help.'

Sam and Brendan made their way back to the farm, climbing over ditches and walls as they went. They spotted the workshop and entered it to find Olafsson hammering a piece of iron. The noise was so deafening the children had to put their fingers in their ears. A scorching fire blazed in the centre of the room, casting dancing shadows on the walls. The heat was extreme. Beads of sweat gathered on Sam's forehead and he hadn't even started to work yet! Shelves on the walls were crammed with all sorts of equipment. The floor was scattered with boxes and barrels of wood, charcoal, nails and other bits of metal.

'Do you want any help?' shouted Brendan at the top of his voice.

Olafsson turned around. 'Find the other piece of this,' he grunted, handing Brendan a broken sword. 'It should be in that box over there.'

The box was full of bits of metal, and especially, bits of swords.

VOYAGE TO VICTORY

9

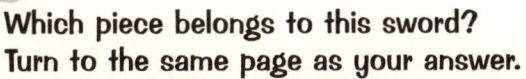
Which piece belongs to this sword?
Turn to the same page as your answer.

VOYAGE TO VICTORY

10

The leaf symbol is the correct answer.

They stepped through the door into the next room which had only one door but with a strange looking contraption high above it. It looked like a pinball machine for giants. The machine was mounted onto the wall and protected by a glass case. A tube went from under the machine to what looked like a lock on the door.

In the centre of the room were two large black ravens perched on two spears, which had been firmly planted in the ground. One of the birds had a red ball in its beak. The other bird opened its beak and began speaking, or rather, squeaking.

'Welcome to Valhalla. My name is Huggin, which means "thought".'

The other raven opened its beak and the small red ball fell to the floor and rolled up to Sam's foot.

'And my name is Muggin, which means "memory",' it croaked.

Brendan stepped forward. 'We're looking for a book,' he said bravely. 'Perhaps you can help?'

'Oh sure!' squeaked Huggin. 'Just go through this door behind me.'

'Only problem is . . . ' croaked Muggin, ' . . . it's locked!'

The two birds squawked loudly as if they were laughing.

'The key is at your foot!' nodded Muggin.

Sam picked up the red ball.

'You must put the ball into one of the holes at the top of the glass case, so that it enters the lock and opens the door!'

The children looked up at the six holes.

'But we can't reach up that high!' complained Sam.

'That's where we come in!' shrieked Huggin, swooping down and plucking the red ball from Sam's fingers. 'Tell me which hole to put it in but remember you only get one chance!'

VOYAGE TO VICTORY

11

Which hole should Huggin drop the ball into?
Turn to the same page as your answer.

VOYAGE TO VICTORY

Age twelve is the correct answer.

Breakfast was handed to the three children by a skinny young Viking. It consisted of some bread, dried fish, blackberries and raspberries and a hollowed out cow's horn filled with water.

'Who needs cornflakes?' smiled Sam. Lisa smiled back. Brendan looked puzzled.

After breakfast, the Vikings raised the sail. It soon billowed with wind and the ship began to toss gently through the waves. Brendan began to tell Sam and Lisa about himself. He and his parents lived with the monks at the monastery.

'What do the monks do?' enquired Lisa.

'Many of them pray all day,' replied Brendan. 'Others work at the farm or as gold- or silver-smiths while some spend the days and nights writing and illuminating holy books.'

'Like the *Book of Time*?' suggested Sam.

'Yes,' said Brendan, 'but the *Book of Time* is no ordinary book. It has special powers. That's why the Vikings want it.'

'What sort of powers?' gasped Lisa.

'I don't know,' replied Brendan. 'I've never actually seen inside it.'

'Well,' said Lisa, 'whatever this book is, it's the only link we have between this time and our time and it's probably our only hope of returning home!' Brendan turned away, obviously upset.

'Don't worry,' she said, touching Brendan's hand. 'We'll get you back home as well.'

'I wonder where the book is?' pondered Sam.

'I'd say he has it,' replied Brendan, pointing to the top of the ship. 'He's the leader. His name is Harold the Hairy Arm.'

Lisa sniggered, 'Which one is Harold the Hairy Arm?'

'The one with the beard, cap, cloak and sword,' said Brendan.

VOYAGE TO VICTORY
13

Can you find Harold the Hairy Arm?
Turn to the same page as his number.

VOYAGE TO VICTORY
14

Fourteen is the smallest number Sam must roll.

Days went by slowly. Every day was the same. Fish to eat and water to drink. The children chatted to each other but mostly sat staring across the sea, bored. The boredom was sometimes broken by the scald who told stories and poems or by a musician who played the flute. Brendan said that the flute was made from the leg bone of a sheep which had holes drilled into it. The Vikings passed the time by playing a board game called hnefatafl and other games with dice. Night-time was the best time because the children could explore the ship, examining the Vikings' possessions and really just being happy to stand up and walk around. They searched for the *Book of Time* on many occasions, but to no avail. Harold the Hairy Arm must have hidden it. Every night he slept on a wooden box. The children presumed it was in there.

One night Sam found a map on the ship. He took it back to his bed and traced the map into Lisa's copy and then returned it. He kept himself busy during the day, consulting his map and compass, although Lisa knew that he hadn't a clue what he was doing. She kept her eye on Harold the Hairy Arm all the time, waiting to catch a glimpse of the *Book of Time* or to see if he left his box unguarded. Of course he never did. In fact, he seemed to spend more and more time every day asleep on it. Sam and Lisa didn't know what they would do with the book if they got it, but it was the only link they had between this time and the future.

It was a cold day and the ship was cruising with the force of a strong wind.

'What are you doing?' Lisa asked Sam, who was writing something in his notebook.

'I've been keeping a track of the number of days we've been at sea,' he answered. 'I put a stroke down for every day.'

VOYAGE TO VICTORY

15

How many days have the children been at sea?
Turn to the same page as your answer.

VOYAGE TO VICTORY
16

Book of Time page sixteen is the correct answer.

'You're good at this,' is code cracking,' praised Brendan. 'Oh, we've had some' practice,' smiled Sam. Lisa returned the smile.

pof ots ece rat
lol umu ch bng
a os ar tto tey
ckot key hfo se
coran tote oe
tnand hu eto vi
htnd iar dhk eg
chda nt og tp h
be rig fu ea nt

VOYAGE TO VICTORY

18

Port number eighteen is the correct answer.

'You may be right,' said Brendan, 'but I still don't see any land.'

Sam grabbed the map back and replaced it in the rucksack. He didn't appreciate Brendan's lack of confidence in him.

'You know they'll take that sack from you when we arrive,' said Brendan.

That night when all the Vikings were asleep, Sam decided that he would hide the rucksack. He took out the scissors and the spool of thread. Using the scissors, he cut a slit into one of the sacks piled up on the ship. Corn spilled out onto the deck and soon the sack was half-empty. He stuffed the rucksack into the sack of corn and then began stitching up the slit using a piece of thread and a fishbone as a needle. When the job was completed, the sack looked as if it had never been touched, except for the pile of corn on the deck. Sam managed to throw most of the grain overboard using his hands as a shovel. The rest, he hoped, would not be noticed by the Vikings the next morning.

He gazed out across the sea. No lights, no sign of land. He returned to bed. Lisa and Brendan were asleep. There was nothing left for them to explore. Sam closed his eyes. Sleep arrived easily.

'Wake up, Sam!' whispered Lisa, shaking him violently.

'OK! OK!' cried Sam. 'No need to kill me! What is it? Can you see land?'

'Not yet,' replied an excited Lisa. 'But I can see something that means we must be near land.'

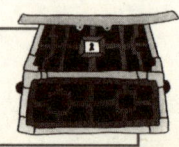

What does Lisa see?
Turn to the same page as that symbol.

VOYAGE TO VICTORY
19

VOYAGE TO VICTORY
20

Twenty objects is the correct answer.

'Hand over the sack, little man!' demanded Scarface. Sam complied with the order. 'Eh? Empty?' mused the Viking, looking in. 'Still, nice stitching on this. I think I'll keep it. Anything else?'

The three children shook their heads and the Viking walked on. Suddenly, the ship rocked. It had started to move. The fifty or so men were pulling at the oars with all their might. A gentle splashing sound could be heard as the oars entered the water, followed by a whoosh as they sliced through the air and then splash again. Splash, whoosh, splash, whoosh . . . Sam lay back against the crate. He was exhausted.

'My name is Brendan,' said the boy, pushing a wisp of hair behind his ear.

Lisa introduced herself and Sam. For the first time all day, she had time to think.

'Who are these people?' asked Lisa. 'And where are we going?'

'Viking raiders,' replied Brendan. 'They're taking us to their homes across the sea. A group attacked our monastery last year but we survived by hiding in the round tower. They came to steal the *Book of Time* and this time they got it.'

'But why?' asked Lisa.

'You mean, you don't know? It's priceless and contains the secrets of the three time zones – the past, the present and the future.'

'What'll happen to us?' frowned Lisa.

'I expect we'll either be killed or turned into slaves,' replied Brendan.

'Oh, is that all!' said Lisa, faking a smile.

She wanted to cry but she also felt that she must be brave. It was the only way to survive this nightmare. She looked over at Sam. He was fast asleep. She pulled an animal skin up over him and lay back herself. Her eyelids felt heavy. Sleep would soon be upon her. Looking up to the sky she hoped that this dream or nightmare or whatever it was would be all over in the morning . . .

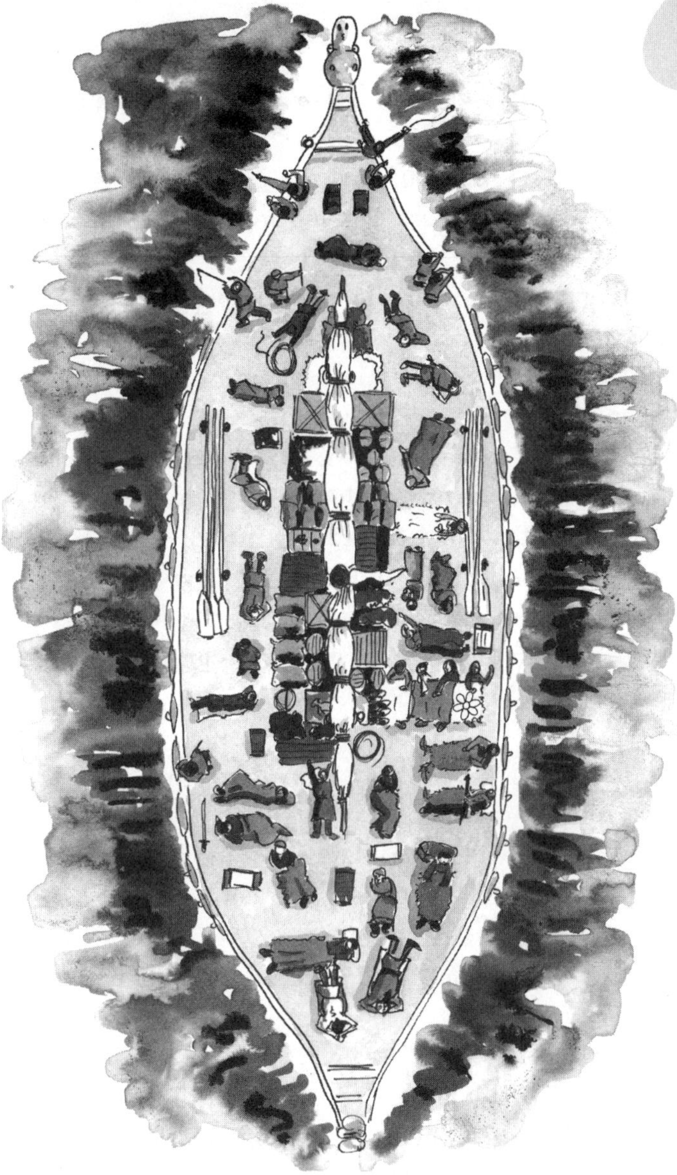

VOYAGE TO VICTORY

21

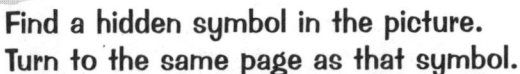
Find a hidden symbol in the picture.
Turn to the same page as that symbol.

Twenty-two flying warriors is the correct answer.

'Let's hide!' shouted Brendan.

'But where?' screamed Lisa, looking around. There was no cover on the ship.

'If we get under one of those trees before they reach the ground, we may not be spotted,' argued Brendan.

He jumped down from the ship, landing on the road in a cloud of dust. Sam and Lisa wasted no time in following. They just about made it under the cover of a tree before the first flying warrior landed on the ship. In seconds, the ship was filled with flying horses and beautiful girls. As swiftly as they landed, they began to fly away, but not empty-handed. One girl put the body of Harold the Hairy Arm onto her horse and flew off with him. She was followed by the others, each of whom carried one of Harold's possessions, including the *Book of Time*. Minutes later the ship was completely empty and the flying warriors were gone.

'Great!' sighed Lisa. 'We've just messed up our best chance of getting that stupid book back!'

The truth was that with the excitement of the strange happenings the children had forgotten all about the book. Silence mixed with devastation hung in the air.

'Sit and sulk if you want,' said Brendan, heading up the road. 'But I'm not giving up yet.'

Sam and Lisa followed the young boy and they walked and walked. The road was dead straight and every patch of it looked the same. Weariness was taking its toll on the children but they still pressed on. Eventually they arrived at a crossroads. A signpost with strange words and symbols pointed in five different directions.

'Which way?' asked Lisa.

'Maybe we'll get help in here,' said Sam, opening up his booklet about Vikings. 'It helped before, why not again?'

VOYAGE TO VICTORY

23

PLACES IN NORSE MYTHOLOGY

MUSPELLHEIM – The land of fire. This region is so hot that only fire giants can survive here. A fire giant named Surt guards the borders of Muspellheim, brandishing his flaming sword.

BIFROST – This is the rainbow bridge that connects Midgard (Earth) with Asgard (home of the gods).

NIFLHEIM – This bleak realm of poisonous ice and fog is the land of the dead and home to the goddess Hel. Legend has it that Hel was banished from Asgard by Odin. Vikings who died of sickness or old age were sent here. Niflheim is also home to Nidogg the dragon who constantly nibbles on the huge roots of the world tree, Yggdrasil.

VALHALLA – Odin's palace where dead warriors are brought back to life and spend their days fighting in preparation for Ragnarok, the end of the world. At Ragnarok Odin's warriors will fight one final battle against the forces of darkness. Only warriors who die an honourable death (that is, in battle) are brought to Valhalla. Female warriors called Valkyries carry the dead and his posessions to Valhalla on their winged horses.

YGGDRASIL – The world tree, whose roots connect all the Viking worlds from Asgard to Midgard and all the way down to Niflheim. When Ragnarok arrives, the tree will shake violently but not fall. After Ragnarok two humans will emerge from the tree to repopulate the world.

Read the page from Sam's booklet and look at the signpost to find out which way to go.
Turn to the same page as the symbol.

24

The leg symbol is the answer to the riddle.

'Surprisingly wise!' mumbled Odin. 'Now let me prove to you my wisdom. Ask me any question and I promise you I will be able to answer it!'

Sam started to think about a really difficult question. He wanted to take this god down a peg or two. He was angry, therefore, when Lisa began asking a question without even consulting him. Afterwards, however, he admitted (to himself, of course) that it was a good question.

'Can you tell me,' said Lisa in her best telephone voice, 'the location of the *Book of Time*?'

'Easy,' replied Odin smugly. 'It's in Harold the Hairy Arms' storage room.'

'Well, anyone would know that,' insisted Lisa. 'Even Muggins there could tell me that!'

The raven screeched loudly, as if deeply offended.

'I bet,' said Lisa, 'that you couldn't tell us exactly where the room is!'

Odin rose to his feet.

'Nothing is too difficult for the great Odin!' he thundered, raising his spear and aiming it at Lisa. She screamed as the spear came hurtling towards her, but instead of passing through her body, it swerved and went around her. Brendan spun around to follow the flying spear. He was flabbergasted to see it hovering in mid-air, halfway down the hall.

'My magic spear, Grungir, will show you the way,' said Odin. 'And it never misses its target.'

As if on command, the spear began moving down the hall. Lisa was still in a state of shock, having seen her life flash before her eyes.

'Let's go!' whispered Sam, grabbing her arm.

VOYAGE TO VICTORY

25

Follow the spear through Valhalla.
What room does it end up in?
Turn to the same page as the number on that room.

VOYAGE TO VICTORY
26

Twenty-six gold objects is the correct answer.

'Thanks,' said the monk, throwing the sack over his shoulder. 'I'm off to put these with the *Book of Time* for safe keeping and I'd advise you to follow me.'

With that he raced out the door.

'What's he talking about?' frowned Sam.

'I haven't a clue,' answered Lisa, 'but let's follow him anyway.'

The children raced towards the door, opened it and went outside. They ground to a sudden halt. Lisa's eyes almost popped out of their sockets. Sam's mouth dropped open. They couldn't believe it. The museum was gone! Sure, the stone houses and churches were still there but now they were made from real stone. The plastic grass was now real grass. In the distance, trees and bushes, hills and mountains could be seen. There was no ceiling above them but, instead, a blue sky streaked with white clouds. A light breeze caused the nearby trees to rustle. Sam and Lisa were stunned.

After what seemed like an eternity of silence, Sam spoke. His voice was jittery, 'Am I dreaming, or do you see what I see?'

'You mean, do I see a real countryside with real mountains and a real sky . . . ' replied Lisa. 'Yes, I do.'

They looked around. There was nobody to be seen. They felt like they were the last people on the planet, or else the first. In their dumbstruck states, they had forgotten about the monk and now he had vanished. All of a sudden panic hit Lisa. She didn't know where she was or how she had got there. Loneliness mixed with fear stirred within her.

'I don't know about you,' she said, her voice quivering, 'but I think we should find that monk. He got us into this mess so perhaps he can get us out. Now, I wonder where he's gone to?'

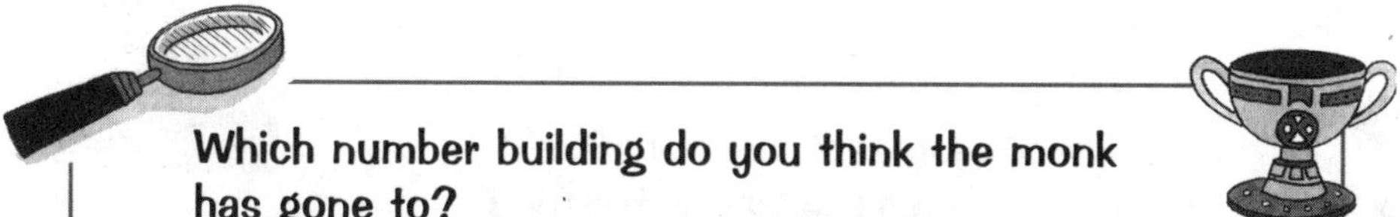

VOYAGE TO VICTORY
27

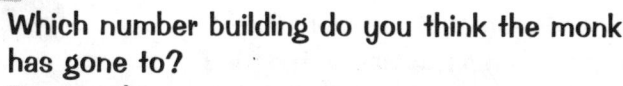
Which number building do you think the monk has gone to?
Turn to the same page as your answer.

VOYAGE TO VICTORY

28

Twenty-eight is the number of the Heritage Museum.

Lisa was stuck in front of a boy called Norman Cranckshaw. Norman had managed to consume a two-litre bottle of fizzy orange before the bus had even left the car park and was now showing the after effects. He spent the whole journey belching and retching into a plastic bag, making Lisa's journey uncomfortable, to say the least. A beeping noise from her rucksack diverted her attention. She hauled the bag onto her knees. What could that be? All that she had packed was some lunch and her copy and pencil. (Miss Fussy had insisted on the more scholarly pupils bringing these!) Lisa was more than surprised to see a walkie-talkie on top of her lunch box.

What's this? she asked herself.

The answer came in the form of a voice from the walkie-talkie, 'COME IN LISA! OVER!'

It was Sam. Lisa pressed the button to reply.

'How did this get here?' she asked.

'Oh! I managed to slip it into your bag when you weren't looking,' crackled the walkie-talkie.

'Where are you sitting?' asked Lisa, squinting her eyes towards the top of the bus.

'Try and work out where I am,' said Sam. 'I'm two seats in front of you, one to the right, two to the front, one to the right, three to the front and one to the left.'

Lisa shook her head wearily. Life was never simple.

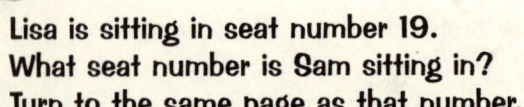

**Lisa is sitting in seat number 19.
What seat number is Sam sitting in?
Turn to the same page as that number.**

VOYAGE TO VICTORY
29

The black arrow is the correct symbol on the horse's teeth.

'Thanks, Sleipnir!' said the children, turning the handle on the door marked with a black arrow. They stepped out into a long wide hall which had doors on both sides. Burning torches illuminated colourful tapestries. Long curtains of white silk hung down from a glittering silver ceiling and were tied to the walls with golden ropes. Angelic music filled the air. On a large throne at the far end of the hall sat a man with a flowing white beard.

'Odin!' whispered Lisa.

Cautiously, they approached the throne. Odin was dressed in armour and a long red cloak and he held a spear in one hand. One eye was covered with a patch, the other seemed to be fixed on the approaching children. Two wolves lay at his feet and two familiar looking ravens sat on his shoulders.

'I've been expecting you,' said Odin.

The ravens began to cackle with laughter. Odin raised his hand, commanding silence.

'This is Valhalla, Hall of the Slain, where the brave fight all day and feast all night in preparation for Ragnarok – the last battle. I am Odin, father of the gods, god of war, death, poetry and, most of all, wisdom. I did, however, pay the price for this wisdom.'

He raised a finger to the patch on his eye.

'What price are you willing to pay?' he asked.

The children didn't know what to say. Receiving no answer, Odin spoke again.

'Prove to me your wisdom and I'll prove to you mine,' he said. 'If you can't, then you must pay the price!'

The wolves growled, displaying pointed fangs.

'Answer this!' commanded Odin. 'What has a bottom at its top?'

Phone a friend? thought Sam.

This wasn't, however, the time or the place.

VOYAGE TO VICTORY
31

The answer to Odin's riddle is one of the above symbols.
Turn to the same page as that symbol.

VOYAGE TO VICTORY
32

Thirty-two days at sea is the correct answer.

More days passed but yet there was still no sign of land. Sam and Lisa were asleep. They had now got into the habit of sleeping during the day and staying awake at night to explore the geography of the ship. Brendan however was still awake. He was sad. He missed his parents and the monks in the monastery. He knew that he might never see them again, although every night he prayed that he would. He had heard stories of people who had been taken captive by Vikings and sold as slaves in other countries.

He was glad however, that Sam and Lisa were with him. They were strange people – from the future of all places! It didn't make sense to him but he believed their story all the same. They came from a strange and wonderful time, a time when people could talk to friends in different countries and even travel across the skies in flying machines. It sounded amazing, but also scary. He didn't know if he would like life in the twenty-first century. The one thing that he did hold on to was the promise that Lisa had made to him.

'Don't worry,' she had said. 'We'll get you back home as well.'

Sam was now awake and rummaging in Lisa's rucksack. He held the compass in his hand and observed it. He then wrote down something on a piece of paper.

'According to my calculations,' he said, 'we should be nearing land soon.'

He showed Brendan the map that he had traced onto a page.

'I've been writing down the directions that we've been travelling in since we left Ireland and it seems to me that we will soon see land. Look!'

He handed Brendan the map. On the map was a list of directions.

'Start at X,' said Sam, 'and follow the directions.'

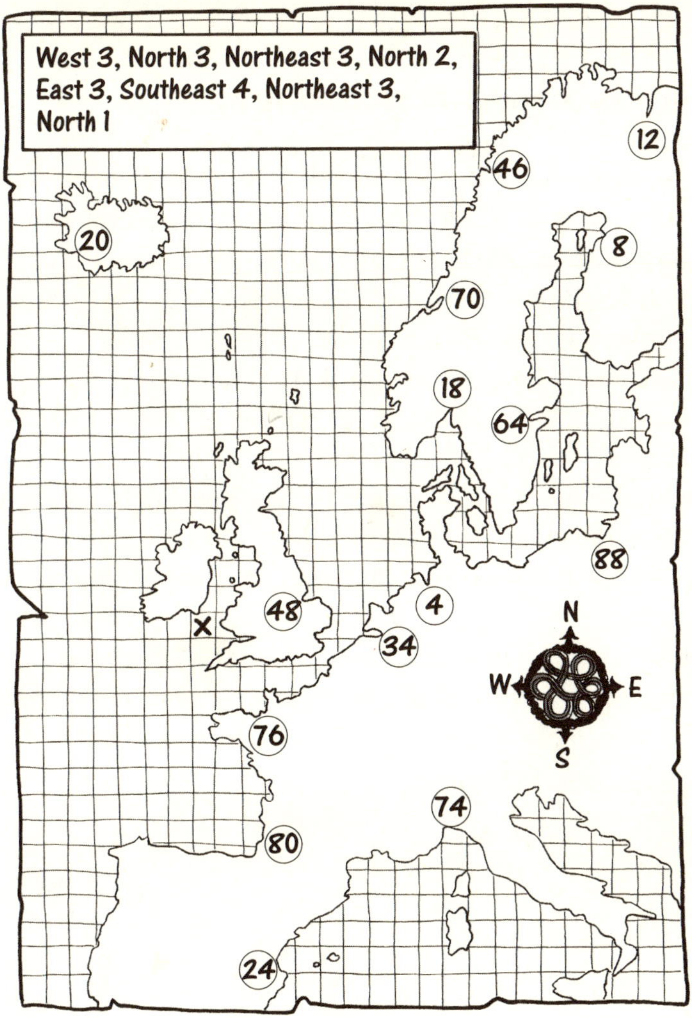

VOYAGE TO VICTORY

33

West 3, North 3, Northeast 3, North 2, East 3, Southeast 4, Northeast 3, North 1

According to the map, what number port will they be arriving at?
Turn to the same page as your answer.

Key number thirty-four is the correct answer.

Fitting the key into the lock, Sam turned it easily. The three children eased the heavy lid up. There it was – the *Book of Time*! Leather-bound and sparkling with brightly coloured stones. Nobody spoke. This moment needed to be savoured.

'At last!' whispered Brendan.

'What now?' asked Sam, his eyes still glued to the book.

Brendan carefully removed the book from the chest and laid it down on the stone floor.

'Let's hope that the answer is inside,' he said, opening the cover. His voice quivered slightly.

The pages were a dull yellow and rather thick, much thicker than paper.

'It's vellum,' Brendan informed them, 'made from calf-skin.'

The writing on the page was obviously done by hand and the letters were a little strange but discernible. Brendan opened up the contents page.

Read through the contents of the <u>Book of Time</u>. What page should they turn to next?

Contents

1. The Monks of Briarhill 8
2. Evening Prayer .. 12
3. Lost Souls 26
4. Old Testament 34
5. Gospels 54
6. Religious Art 84
7. Time Travel 96
8. A Monk's Vision 100
9. Scribes 106

Warning!
Important parts of this book may be in code.

VOYAGE TO VICTORY
36

Person number thirty-six is the correct answer.

Sam's hands were being tied by a Viking.

'Leave him alone, you knucklehead!' screamed Lisa running over.

She punched the Viking on the arm. He spun around and grabbed her.

'So you're not dead!' he grinned. 'Maybe we'll take you as well. My wife would love a present like you.'

Lisa screamed as the man bound her wrists tightly together. She was then connected to Sam with another rope.

'Come on!' snarled the Viking, tugging the rope.

'Knucklehead,' mumbled Lisa stumbling after him.

The monastery was now in ruins. Black smoke rose up from battered-looking houses and churches, whose contents were scattered all over the grass. Children were crying in doorways. Women tended to their injured husbands, many of whom looked beyond recuperation. Frightened monks clutched their rosary beads as they watched their most precious possessions being taken away. The Vikings loaded the gold and silver valuables into sacks along with holy books and provisions such as food, wine, water and animal skins. Then the procession of Viking raiders marched off towards the sea, leaving behind a plundered and scarred monastery.

Stumbling uncertainly along with them Sam and Lisa noticed that they weren't the only prisoners. Some men were also tied up and being forced to leave their homes.

They headed southwest from the monastery. Rounding a hill with a large tree on top, they then headed southeast. They crossed over the river and followed it to a crossroads. Going straight through the crossroads, they carried on for a short distance before crossing back over the river and heading for the forest. They took the first left and then the second right.

VOYAGE TO VICTORY
37

Which inlet did they arrive at?
Turn to the same page as your answer.

VOYAGE TO VICTORY
38

Recipe number thirty-eight is the correct answer.

When the meal was ready, the table was set. Freyda opened one of the barrels. It was full of home-made beer. Knut returned with two other men. Lisa recognised them from the ship. They sat down and ate a lot and drank even more. The more they drank, the more they talked. Lisa took her food to the other table but she could still hear the conversation.

'Harold the Hairy Arm is dying. His stomach hasn't healed from the wound he received in that monastery.'

'How do you know his stomach hasn't healed?'

'We fed him onion porridge and then waited a while. When we smelled his wound, we could smell onion through it. That means that his stomach has been pierced. He will die very soon.'

'What are we going to do?'

'I don't know. I just don't know!'

Freyda approached Lisa.

'You look tired,' she said. 'Go to bed and get some sleep.'

'Tired' was an understatement. Lisa was absolutely exhausted!

As she snuggled up under the covers, she felt guilty. She shouldn't be going to sleep when Sam and Brendan were out there, possibly in danger. She wanted to go and look for them but her legs said 'no!' She hoped they were all right. How was she going to get out of here? How was she going to get home? How was she . . ?

Her eyes closed and she fell into a deep dark sleep.

Turn back to page 95.

VOYAGE TO VICTORY
39

Forty coins is the correct answer.

'My wife will be happy with that,' smiled Olaf, taking the silk.

They continued walking past different stalls selling a wide variety of goods. You could buy glass, wine, spices, furs, jewellery, amber, weapons, ropes, walrus ivory, pottery, salt and even slaves! The merchants accepted silver coins or bits and pieces of silver called 'hack silver' or, sometimes, they just swapped items with other buyers.

'Now I want to do a bit of selling myself,' said Olaf to the children. 'I have a silver arm ring, a silver brooch and a silver necklace that my wife doesn't want anymore. I want to exchange them for coins.'

He stopped at a jewellery stall. A fat merchant had all sorts of jewellery laid out on blue cloth. Olaf produced his items of jewellery and asked the merchant how many coins he would give for them. The merchant examined the items and seemed genuinely pleased. He said that he would give two silver coins per ortugar. The weight of the jewellery was measured in ortugars. One ortugar was equivalent to about eight grammes. The jewellery was put on one side of a small hand-held scales and small iron weights were put on the other side until the scales balanced. Each iron weight had dots on it. One dot meant one ortugar. Firstly, the merchant weighed the arm ring. Sam and Brendan took note of how many ortugars it weighed. The brooch was then weighed and finally, the necklace. Sam added up the three weights in his head.

'Now, the merchant said that he would give two silver coins per ortugar,' he said to himself.

**Look at the weight of each item.
How many silver coins should the merchant pay Olaf?**

VOYAGE TO VICTORY
41

42

Forty-two is the answer to the rainbow puzzle.

The coloured light was so dazzling that the children squinted their eyes. Approaching the base of the rainbow, the ship slowed down. As it gently entered the tower of colour, night disappeared and Sam, Lisa and Brendan turned bright green. They looked like little green aliens from a cartoon. Sam stretched out his arm until his hand turned yellow. Brendan did the same, except in the opposite direction and his hand turned blue. Lisa ran to the edge of the ship and turned orange. With all the excitement of turning themselves into different colours, the children didn't notice that the ship was rising up into the air. Lisa looked over the edge and gasped when she realised that the sea was a long way down. The ship was now floating in the air and slowly rising up towards the top of the rainbow. The children busied themselves with running from one end of the ship to the other, changing colour. Soon, however, the fun was over and the ship emerged at the top of the rainbow and continued to move along it in a horizontal direction.

'This just gets weirder and weirder,' exclaimed Sam.

Above them was a bright blue sky with white fluffy clouds. Below them was blackness except for the river of colours which they were travelling along. The children raced to the front of the ship. The rainbow seemed to be leading up to a strip of 'land' which was floating in the air. As they got closer they recognised the strip of land as a road. Beautiful green trees flourished on both sides. Eventually, the ship pulled up to this dusty road and stopped. The rest of the rainbow continued under the road into the darkness.

'Oh no!' shrieked Lisa, pointing to the sky.

Dozens of female armour-clad warriors with swords, shields, axes and spears were approaching the ship. They flew through the sky on flying white horses with feathery wings. In seconds, they would be upon them.

VOYAGE TO VICTORY

43

How many flying warriors are there?
Turn to the same page as your answer.

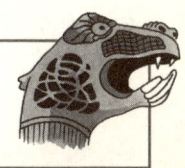

Person number forty-four bought Sam and Brendan.

'My name is Olaf,' said the Viking to the two boys, 'and you two are now mine. You cost me a lot so you'd better be worth it. I'll have various jobs for you to do every day. Work hard and you'll be rewarded with good food and a warm dry bed.'

Sam and Brendan followed Olaf to the edge of the town, to a little farm. There was a long wooden house surrounded by smaller stone buildings, all with thatched roofs. Olaf directed the children to one of them.

'You will live here,' he said, 'with the other slaves.'

He then showed the boys around his farm. He pointed out a slave who was ploughing a field using a wooden plough. He showed them the vegetable field, the rubbish heap, the animal house and the storage house. Olaf then led them to a tiny building, which was the toilet. Inside was a wooden seat with a hole in it. Under the hole was a large pot. The smell was disgusting.

'You must empty this pot every morning,' said Olaf.

He walked on, beckoning the children to follow.

'Ugh!' moaned Sam. 'Hasn't the flush been invented yet?'

Brendan raised his eyebrows.

'Forget it!' sighed Sam, running after Olaf who was now halfway up one of the fields.

'Up there,' said Olaf, 'is a field of cows. Some of them escaped last night. I want you to go and see how many are missing. There should be forty.'

'I get the feeling that perhaps I'm not cut out for farm work,' said Sam, looking down at his feet. He had just stepped in cow manure!

Brendan laughed, 'You haven't got much of a choice! Now, let's count these cows.'

VOYAGE TO VICTORY
45

How many cows are missing?
Turn to the same page as your answer.

VOYAGE TO VICTORY

46

Person number forty-six is the correct answer.

When the Vikings weren't rowing the ship, they sat eating and drinking and let the sail do the work. Some of the Vikings had been injured in the attack on the monastery. Harold the Hairy Arm looked very bad. His bandage was changed every day but he didn't seem to be getting any better. Often the Vikings drank too much and became drunk, vomiting over the side of the ship. Others caught fish on lines and in nets. Nobody paid any attention to Sam, Lisa or Brendan. At about midday they were handed three bowls of something that looked like fish stew.

'Ugh!' cried Lisa. 'I'm not eating that!'

Brendan began eating and dipping pieces of bread into his bowl.

'It's actually very nice,' he proclaimed.

Lisa wasn't convinced but hunger got the better of her and she realised that he was right – it was tasty! The children chatted all day, educating each other about the ninth and the twenty-first centuries.

As night began to fall, a scald sat down near the children. A scald is a Viking storyteller. He began to relate to his shipmates a wonderful Viking saga about Thor, the god of thunder, and his visit to Utgard, the land of the giants. By the end of the story it was dark and most of the Vikings lay back and fell into deep slumbers. Soon the whole ship was asleep, all except the children.

'I'm stiff from sitting down all day,' moaned Sam. 'How about a bit of exploring? My legs could do with a stretch.'

Lisa and Brendan agreed. They tiptoed around the sleeping bodies.

'I think I see the *Book of Time*,' whispered Brendan.

Find the <u>Book of Time</u>.
On the book is a symbol.
Turn to the same page as that symbol.

VOYAGE TO VICTORY
47

VOYAGE TO VICTORY
48

Seat number forty-eight is the correct answer.

Lisa was just about to shout up to Sam when her intentions were drowned out by fifty screaming children. They cheered and clapped as the bus pulled into the car park of the Heritage Museum.

'At last!' groaned Norman, removing his head from the plastic bag.

Miss Fussy stood up and began her usual shushing and flapping of hands to subdue the children. When silence was finally restored, she began to speak.

'Now, children, listen up,' she said. 'We'll all take a tour of the museum and then break for lunch at one. We're going to split up into groups. The front half of the bus, that's the first six rows, will come with me and the rest of the bus will go with the tour guide, Mr Snore. And remember, best behaviour at all times!'

Miss Fussy instructed her group, which included Sam, to follow her into the museum. As Sam exited the bus, he turned to give Lisa a reassuring wink and held up his walkie-talkie. She understood the message. Miss Fussy handed each child a map of the museum before they all headed for the Stone Age section.

Once there, she began her lecture. 'Over here, you can see the remains of some of the tools used by primitive man . . .'

Blah! Blah! Blah! thought Sam.

He was bored already and, although he wouldn't admit it to anybody else but himself, he missed Lisa. Sam slipped in behind a pillar.

'Where are you, Lisa?' he whispered into the walkie-talkie.

A faint voice crackled back, 'I'm in the Viking section.'

'Right,' replied Sam. 'I'm coming to get you!'

Sam looked at his map and then all around him.

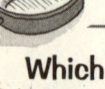

**Which number door should Sam take?
Turn to the same page as that number.**

VOYAGE TO VICTORY

49

Wicklow County Council
County Library Services

50

Hole number fifty is the correct answer.

The children watched the ball fall down the tube and into the lock. CLICK! The door swung open.

'See you soon!' squawked the ravens as the children left the room.

They were now in another square stone room with five open doors.

'Let's try this one,' suggested Brendan.

The next room also had many doors but only one was open. The third room was similar with only one open door. Although they passed through many oddly shaped rooms with many doors, there was always only one door open and therefore only one way to go.

'Let's hope this is leading us somewhere and not round in circles,' said Lisa.

As they progressed, Lisa noticed a little fly buzzing around above them. She tried to swoosh it away but it avoided her clumsy swing. Instead, it merely hovered above them as if observing their actions. It was starting to annoy her. She made another swipe at it.

'It's only a fly, Lisa!' said Sam. 'After all we've seen and been through, you'd think a fly would be the least of your worries.'

'It's giving me the creeps, that's all!' retorted Lisa.

'Scaredy cat!' jeered Sam.

'Oh come on, you two!' urged Brendan, flicking his hair back, 'We haven't got time for this!'

**Which room did the children end up in?
Turn to the same page as the number on that room.**

VOYAGE TO VICTORY

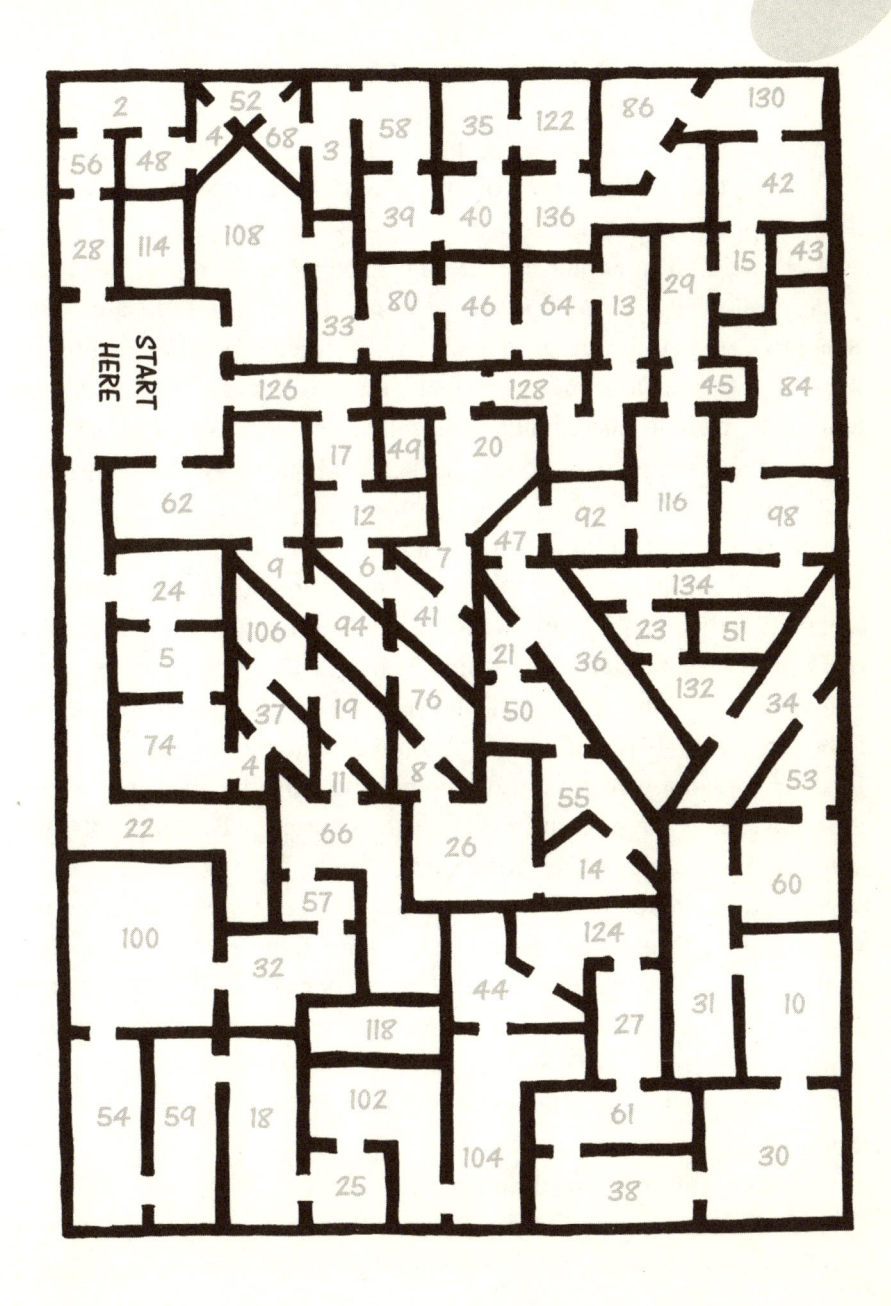

51

VOYAGE TO VICTORY

52

Person number fifty-two is the correct answer.

Lisa didn't see Sam sneaking up behind her.

'You frightened the life out of me!' she scolded, as Sam grabbed her arm and pulled her aside.

'Let's do a bit of exploring!' he suggested, already moving away.

Lisa followed her friend into a section entitled 'Land of Saints and Scholars'. A small group of visitors had gathered around an exhibit in the centre of the floor and were listening to a tour guide. Something that the tour guide said caught Sam's attention. He stopped to listen.

'. . . the most valuable book in the world currently valued at four million euro.'

Money always caught Sam's attention.

'. . . a lot of money, I hear you say, but this book was also priceless in the seventh century. It was written over three centuries by the monks of Briar Hill Monastery. It has always been called the *Book of Time*, and legend has it that the book is the key to the past, present and future, although scientists regard this as pure myth. The monks kept the book in their round tower for safe keeping and now it sits here in our museum under high security. This glass case is bullet proof and connected to a series of sensitive alarms.'

As Sam attempted to push into the group to get a closer look, a loud voice boomed through the speakers that were mounted on the museum walls, 'Ladies and gentlemen, may I have your attention please. There has been a breach of security within the museum. All visitors are requested to report to the main entrance immediately!'

Chaos reigned as people began rushing about in this direction and that.

'What's going on?' asked Sam.

'I don't know,' replied Lisa, 'but that monk certainly looks suspicious.' She pointed into the panicking crowd.

VOYAGE TO VICTORY
53

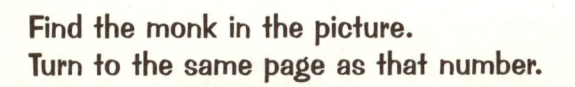

Find the monk in the picture.
Turn to the same page as that number.

VOYAGE TO VICTORY

54

Box number fifty-four is the correct answer.

Lisa returned with the box of gifts.

'Great!' exclaimed Freyda. 'Now tidy up the house. My husband, Knut, will go mad if he sees it in this state.'

She's obviously never heard of feminism, Lisa thought.

The house was very long but had no rooms inside. It was all just one big room. At one end were the beds and, instead of wardrobes, clothes were stored in wooden chests. There were two large tables. On one of them was an ironing board made from whalebone. Lisa had seen Freyda ironing clothes on this, using a big lump of heated glass. At the other end of the room was a large loom with a partially completed tapestry. Beside this, three small wooden barrels stood by a wall. Oil lamps provided the only light in the house as there were no windows. In the middle of the house was a large fire which remained lit all the time. Pots hung from the rafters just over the fire. Sometimes the place became so smoky that Lisa's eyes watered because there was no chimney, just a small hole in the roof.

The two pet dogs had knocked all the firewood down so Lisa stacked it up again. After that, she hung up a pile of wet clothes on a clothesline on one wall. She then gathered up bits of food, rubbish and bones from the floor and dumped them into a hole in the ground at the back of the house. Her body felt like jelly after all her work but just as she was about to sit down, Freyda entered.

'Now, we must cook something nice for Knut,' she said. 'Choose one of the recipes on the wall. Make sure it's something with carrots and mushrooms, but he doesn't like apples or onions.'

'A woman's work is never done,' Lisa's mother used to say.

Lisa now knew what she meant.

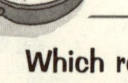

**Which recipe should Lisa choose?
Turn to the same page as that number.**

VOYAGE TO VICTORY
55

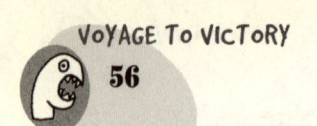

Fifty-six coins is the correct answer.

Olaf put the coins into his leather bag.

'Well done!' he said, slapping the two boys on the back.

Sam wanted to have a look around the town but their journey home took them back the same route. By the time they reached the farm it was almost dark.

'Off to bed!' ordered Olaf. 'I'll see you in the morning.'

Sam and Brendan were left standing alone in the darkness. The other slaves were probably already in bed.

'He obviously trusts us not to run away,' whispered Sam.

'He doesn't have to trust us,' replied Brendan. 'It's not as if we're going to try to escape back to Ireland!'

'Want to bet?' whispered Sam, walking back towards the town.

Brendan raced after him. 'Where are you going?' he asked.

'I'm going into town to find Lisa and then find that *Book of Time* and, hopefully, figure out a way to get home,' said Sam.

Soon they arrived in the town. The place was relatively quiet. The night had grown even darker. Shortly it would be impossible to see. A few people passed by but nobody took any notice of the children.

'How are we going to find Lisa?' Brendan asked.

'Like this,' replied Sam, approaching an old woman.

'We have a message from Olaf for that man who bought the young slave girl this morning,' said Sam confidently. 'Do you know where he lives?'

The woman pointed up the town. 'It's the house with the dead cow above the door,' she said.

'What's the story with the dead cow?' Sam asked Brendan.

'Disgusting, isn't it? I think it's a sacrifice to one of their gods.'

VOYAGE TO VICTORY
57

Turn back to page 95.

VOYAGE TO VICTORY

58

Person number fifty-eight is the correct answer.

'Let's follow him,' suggested a now rather excited Sam. Perhaps museums weren't so boring after all.

'Oh, maybe he just works here,' replied Lisa, doubting herself. 'You know, one of those guys who gets paid to dress up, to give the place a sense of realism.'

'You mean you think that hair cut was part of the job requirement!' sneered Sam. 'I don't think so!'

Lisa shook her head, 'Who said sarcasm was the cleverest form of wit?'

Sam began running in the direction of the monk.

Oh, why not? thought Lisa, following in his footsteps. The chase continued towards the west wing of the museum where houses and churches made of imitation stone stood upright on plastic grass. The sound of chanting monks poured through speakers mounted on the walls, to give atmosphere. The children followed the monk into one of the fake churches. Inside was surprisingly realistic. It was even cold and damp. Two rows of stone benches led up to an altar of stone. Slender shafts of light slanted in through narrow windows, reflecting on the many imitation gold objects scattered around the church.

The monk turned and stared wide-eyed at the children. He held a brown sack in his hand and he looked very confused. Sam and Lisa were equally perplexed. The monk began to speak.

'Look,' he said, 'you either help me get all the gold into this bag or else clear off. I haven't got much time!'

Sam and Lisa looked at each other.

'He must be the security breach,' whispered Sam.

'Hardly,' replied Lisa. 'What's he doing stealing this imitation gold? It's probably only plastic!'

'Perhaps he's off his rocker!' smiled Sam.

'Let's help him anyway. He looks a bit frightened,' said Lisa.

VOYAGE TO VICTORY
59

How many gold objects are there?
Turn to the same page as your answer.

VOYAGE TO VICTORY

60

The white arrow is the correct symbol.

Sam, Lisa and Brendan pushed open the wooden door. They stepped into a large stone room with a high ceiling, which was made up of old Viking shields and spears. Some were broken, others were blood-spattered. The children glanced nervously around but the room was empty. Soft light trickled in through the narrow windows behind them, illuminating the strangest looking wall that the children had ever seen. There were twenty wooden doors on the wall, in four rows of five. Narrow ladders led up to each row. Each door had a symbol on it.

'Eh . . . which one?' asked Brendan.

'I dunno,' replied Sam. 'Let's try this one!'

Lisa and Brendan watched him open one of the bottom doors and disappear inside. A few seconds later he appeared through one of the doors on the top row. He looked baffled.

'Try another one!' shouted Brendan.

Sam opened another door and went in, only to reappear, this time on the second row.

'Let me try!' said Brendan, opening one of the bottom doors. Seconds later a door opened on the third row and Brendan stepped out.

'This is going to take forever,' thought Lisa.

She began to study the symbols on the doors. It didn't take her long to realise which door was the one they should take.

'OK, boys. I think I know which door to take,' she shouted proudly.

Which door should they take?
Turn to the same page as that symbol.

VOYAGE TO VICTORY

61

VOYAGE TO VICTORY
62

Inlet number sixty-two is the correct answer.

When they arrived at the inlet, a magnificent wooden longship awaited them. It rocked gently in the waters. A tall mast supported a sail which was rolled up. Carved into the prow of the ship was a fearsome-looking serpent's head, causing the vessel to seem alive. Oars dangled from the ship's sides like weary arms and a few colourful shields hung over the sides.

The calmness of the inlet was disturbed by the return of the Vikings to their ship. Suddenly the place became a hive of activity. Bags of loot, corn and food were loaded onto the vessel. Vikings waded out into the shallow water carrying precious books, jugs and barrels of water and wine and all sorts of other stolen goods. Some live sheep and goats were also being put aboard.

The Viking, whom Lisa now called Knucklehead, remained on the shore with his captives, watching his fellow warriors load the ship. When this was completed he tugged at the rope and stepped into the water. The children gasped – the water was freezing. It wasn't deep but by the time they reached the ship the level was almost up to their rucksacks. Sam was afraid he would fall over because he couldn't use his hands to balance himself. Knucklehead cut the ropes, leaving raw imprints on the children's wrists. He grabbed Lisa under the arms and lifted her up high above his head where another gruff-looking Viking took her aboard. Sam was hoisted up next.

The children looked around them. The centre of the ship was loaded with goods. At both sides the Vikings were removing their helmets and hanging up their shields. They now sat in rows, holding the large oars in their hands. The adult prisoners were being made to do the same. Sam and Lisa hoped they wouldn't have to!

'Right,' said Knucklehead. 'You can make yourselves useful. This is a list of my provisions. Check that I've got everything!'

VOYAGE TO VICTORY
63

There is one thing on the list that Knucklehead doesn't have. What is it?
Turn to the same page as that symbol.

Sixty-four days is the correct answer.

'Well done,' said Thor, 'but I haven't time to play games all night. I have a job to do.'

With that, he raised his hammer in the air and looked upwards. A boom of thunder exploded in the sky followed by flashes of lightning. The noise caused the sleeping Vikings to jump to attention and soon the ship was crawling with activity as the crew prepared for a storm. The children looked around. Thor had vanished and Harold the Hairy Arm was gathering the *Book of Time* under his cloak to protect it from the rain which had started to fall.

Bewildered, the children stumbled back to their crate, as the sail was opened out and pinned to both sides of the ship. Poles were erected underneath turning the sail into a tent, to keep everybody dry. Small lamps provided some feeble light under the canvas. The rain beat down heavily as the children reflected on their encounter with Thor.

'What exactly was that?' asked Sam.

'A dream?' suggested Brendan.

'I don't know what just happened there,' concluded Lisa, 'but I do know one thing. That book has powers not to be messed with.'

After a while Brendan contented himself by playing with three small dice. Sam grabbed a nearby lamp and eyed one of the dice with curiosity.

'I picked them up last night,' Brendan informed him. 'They're made from walrus ivory and drilled with holes to mark spots . . . let's play!'

He rolled a six, a five and a two.

What is the smallest number Sam must roll to beat Brendan's score?
Turn to the same page as your answer.

VOYAGE TO VICTORY
65

Viking number sixty-six is the correct answer.

Sam and Brendan stepped quietly between the sleeping bodies. The sounds of snores and the odd grunt or mumble fractured the air. Scarface was lying on Lisa's rucksack. Sam opened one of the side pockets, his hand trembling with fear. Slowly he pulled out Brendan's silver cross and rosary beads. The boy's face lit up. Then, without making a sound, they tiptoed back to their crate.

'Thanks,' said Brendan. 'It's all I have to remind me of my family. This cross belonged to my twin brother who died four years ago at the age of eight. My parents said that if I carry it everywhere with me, then my brother will look down on me and keep me safe.'

'Were they your parents in the round tower?' asked Sam.

Brendan nodded his head. His big eyes became glassy with tears.

Bad question, thought Sam.

In an attempt to cheer the boy up and change the subject, Sam grabbed the rucksack. He showed Brendan the contents – the camera, the walkie-talkies, the compass and the other objects. The boy became engrossed. He asked Sam about life in the future. Sam told him about cars and aeroplanes, hairdryers, televisions, computers, phones, banks and schools. Brendan was fascinated and as soon as Sam had answered one question he asked another. They sat up talking for hours on end.

The night sky began to grow brighter, the stars began to fade and soon the sun peeped up over the horizon. One of the sheep bleated from a crate further up the ship. A Viking yawned. It was morning and slowly the ship filled with movement and noises.

'Now it's my turn to ask the questions,' smiled Sam. 'You haven't told me anything about yourself. I don't even know what age you are . . . sorry, actually, I do know how old you are!'

VOYAGE TO VICTORY
67

What age is Brendan?
If you don't know, read page 66 again.
Turn to the same page as your answer.

The house is the correct symbol.

As it turned out, the children didn't have to look very far for Harold the Hairy Arm. In fact, it was Harold who found them – sort of.

As they searched the town for the other stone that would indicate Harold's house, they saw the lights of burning torches approaching. Taking cover behind a low wall, they watched a procession of people, maybe thirty or forty, walking slowly with burning torches. The procession was led by a horse-drawn wagon. In the wagon, lying on furs, was the body of Harold the Hairy Arm!

'He's dead!' gasped Lisa.

'This must be his funeral,' whispered Sam.

The children watched the people pass by. Many of them were carrying objects like barrels, pots, shields, swords, spears, clothes and other possessions, including one which all three children recognised – the *Book of Time*!

'Where are they going?' asked Brendan.

'I don't know,' replied Lisa, 'but wherever the book goes, we go!'

At the end of the procession was another horse-drawn cart, but this one was covered with cloth.

'Follow me,' urged Sam, running after the procession.

Brendan and Lisa watched him crawl into the back of the moving cart. He then stuck his head out from under the cover and beckoned the children to follow. A few seconds later, all three children were travelling under cover!

**Who has the Book of Time?
Turn to the same page as the number of that person.**

VOYAGE TO VICTORY
69

Room number seventy is the correct answer.

The children ran in pursuit and found the spear planted into a small wooden door. They stopped to catch their breaths. They were all panting heavily.

'That Grungir would make a great fitness instructor,' puffed Sam.

They entered a small narrow room. The walls were lined with shelves, all of which were crammed with various objects. The room was littered with crates, barrels, skins, pots, jewellery, silk, jars, helmets, bread, beer and many other things. The children searched frantically for the *Book of Time*, but it was nowhere to be seen. Brendan lifted up a golden chalice from a crate.

'Hey!' he said. 'This is from our church back home!'

The sound of the word 'home' brought sweet sensations to all three children, but it was the book that was needed and, unfortunately, it was the one thing that they couldn't find.

'Over here!' shouted Lisa.

She was crouched down on the floor and had pulled out a heavy chest from under a deerskin.

'I recognise that!' smiled Brendan. 'Harold the Hairy Arm never let it leave his sight the whole time on the ship.'

'Yeah!' laughed Sam. 'He even slept on it! I bet the book is inside!'

'Oh, top marks, Sherlock!' jeered Lisa.

The chest, however, wouldn't open. It was locked. The children scanned the room quickly. A bunch of keys hung above the door. Using a spear, Sam lifted the bunch of keys down.

'Funny looking keys!' muttered Sam, as he examined the bunch.

Which key fits the lock on the chest?
Turn to the same page as the number on that key.

VOYAGE TO VICTORY
71

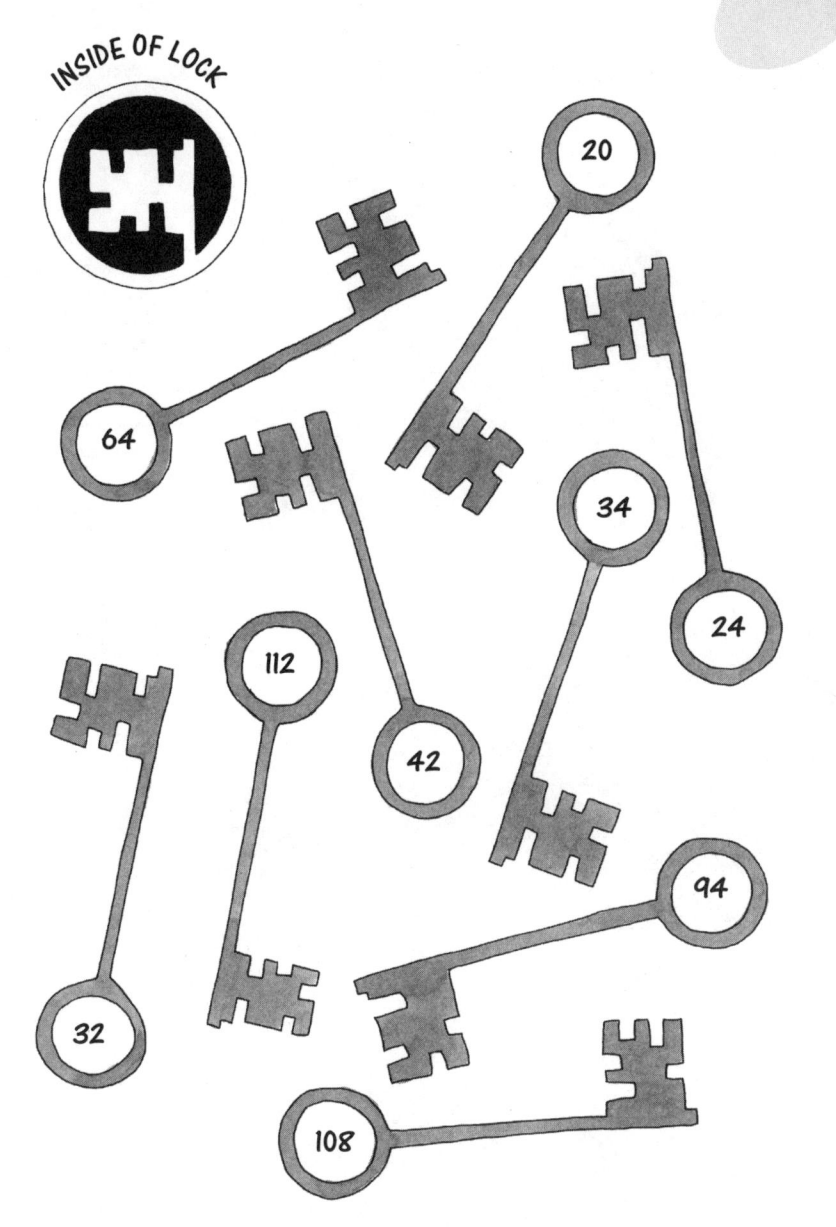

INSIDE OF LOCK

20
64
34
24
112
42
32
94
108

VOYAGE TO VICTORY

B 72

Book of Time page seventy-two is the correct answer.

'So far so good,' said Lisa. 'Now, what does this say?'

nobody will plant cedars nobody jeers cats undressed rats hearts break only on kitchen objects musty commercials frollick with mats heavily placed any daytime white witches young artists elevate having turned to see pigs die at age sixteen

VOYAGE TO VICTORY
74

Book number seventy-four is the correct answer.

All of a sudden the tower fell silent. The candles were quenched, shrouding the place in blackness. Silence lasted for a short while before the air was filled with the war cries of men and the screams of women and children. Crying, shouting, the clanging of metal on stone, crashing and banging and the sounds of violent destruction could be heard outside. Soon the smell of smoke and the crackle of burning invaded the tower, but nobody moved inside.

'Vikings,' whispered the boy to Lisa. 'We'll be safe in here. The tower has no door and the windows are boarded up. It's the people outside that I'm worried about. The tower isn't big enough to hold everybody.'

The sounds of chaos outside continued for a while and gradually died down to a sinister silence. The people inside the tower remained like statues. Sam's legs ached. Lisa wiped the perspiration from her brow. Above their heads somebody stirred. The woman re-lit her candle.

'They're gone!' whispered the boy. 'We've survived again!'

A voice called down from above them, 'I'm opening up!'

It was the monk whom they had met earlier. The window boards were loosened and shafts of light filtered down into the tower. What happened next took place in an instant. As soon as the monk unboarded the window, there was a shout, the sound of a struggle and then a thud and, all of a sudden, a large bearded man wearing a helmet came thundering down the stairs. He held a sword in one hand and a flaming torch in the other. The monks dropped to their knees in prayer. The man pounced on the intruder, only to be flung aside, crashing into Lisa. Banging her head sharply off the stone wall, she fell to the ground, unconscious. When she opened her eyes again, she realised that she was lying on the grass outside the tower. The first thought that raced through her head was to find Sam. Where was he?

VOYAGE TO VICTORY
75

Find Sam.
Turn to the same page as his number.

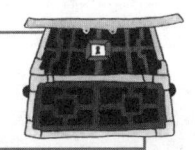

Seventy-six minutes is the correct answer.

Sam and Lisa followed their teacher back to the class who were gathered around, yes, you've guessed it – the Book of Time.

'Now children, here's a story to tell your parents tonight,' Mr Snore began. 'The security alert that we've just had was, in fact, a foiled attempt to steal our most valuable artefact – the *Book of Time*. Three men, dressed as cleaners, have just been arrested in the museum for carrying dangerous firearms and explosives. It seems that the men were planning to hold the museum up and make off with our precious *Book of Time*. They might have succeeded, had our security guards not been tipped off minutes before the raid was due to take place. The thieves were therefore arrested before any disturbance was caused. We are extremely grateful to the mystery person who tipped us off. I say "mystery" because this man has since disappeared into thin air. The funny thing is that one of our security guards described him as being dressed like a monk with a shaved head! He was last seen running towards our reconstructed monastery, but then disappeared without a trace. Whoever he is, we are extremely grateful.'

Sam looked at Lisa. She returned an equally bewildered look.

'Perhaps,' laughed Mr Snore, 'it has something to do with the inscription at the front of the book: *This book shall be eternally protected by the past, the present and the future.*'

'So what you're saying,' interrupted Sam, 'is that this monk travelled from the past to our present to protect the book from being stolen?'

Some of the children giggled.

'I was only joking,' laughed Mr Snore.

He looked over to Miss Fussy. 'Kids, eh?'

All the children were looking at Sam and giggling. His face had turned a deep shade of red.

Lisa, however, comforted him with her own opinion.

'You know, Sam,' she whispered, 'I think you could be right!'

VOYAGE TO VICTORY
77

Multiply the number of people in the picture by 10 and add 4.
Turn to the same page as that number.

VOYAGE TO VICTORY

78

Book of Time page seventy-eight is the correct answer.

'This one looks a bit tricky,' exclaimed Lisa.

VOYAGE TO VICTORY

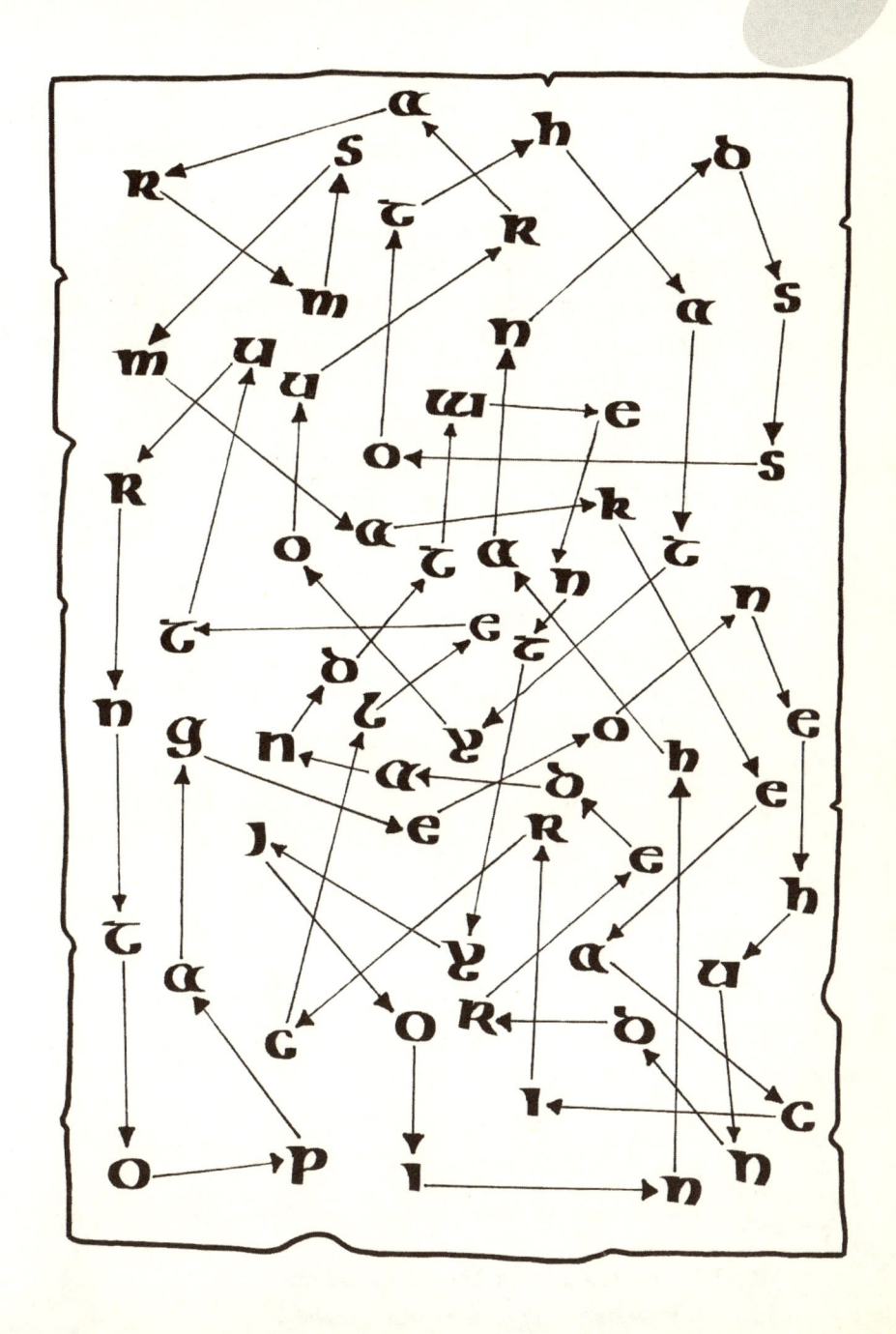

The triangle symbol is on the book.

Brendan opened the book. A shaft of blinding white light shot up into the sky. The shaft broadened and intensified to such a brightness that the children couldn't see. They shielded their eyes and stumbled backwards. The light, however, seemed to be dimming revealing the outline of a man standing within. As the light became duller, the shape became more discernible. A large Viking warrior, clad in armour and brandishing a large hammer, stood before them. Looking out under bushy eyebrows were two sparkling red eyes, like ruby marbles. The bulbous nose would have dominated his face, had it not been for his bushy beard that grew like a wild plant from under his nose, spreading out in all direction down as far as his belly. He remained still, almost lifeless, looking at the children. Sam looked around. All the other Vikings were still sound asleep. He decided to be brave.

'Who are you?' he asked.

The warrior answered in a deep voice, and although his beard moved, you couldn't see his mouth.

'Thor,' he said.

The children looked at each other.

'Where have you come from?' asked Lisa.

'Far away,' Thor replied.

'How far?' asked Sam, trying not to sound cheeky. He was genuinely interested.

'You tell me,' said Thor. 'Valhalla is halfway between here and home. Bifrost is halfway between here and Valhalla. If it takes sixteen days to get to Bifrost, how many days will it take to get home?'

What is the answer to Thor's question?
Turn to the same page as your answer.

VOYAGE TO VICTORY

81

VOYAGE TO VICTORY

82

Book of Time page eighty-two is the correct answer.

Lisa shook her head in bewilderment as she tried to work out the next set of instructions. Brendan was equally perplexed.

'Perhaps,' smiled Sam, 'the border at the top and bottom of the page is a clue.'

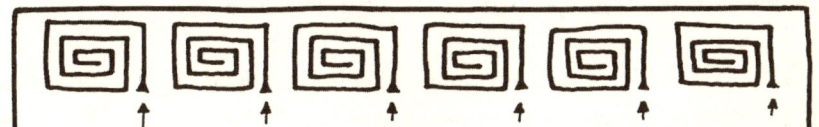

VOYAGE TO VICTORY

83

idesolcseyeruoy
mnepouoynehwotg
ayrutwonerehtgn
goniednaberdeni
iutghteen!!nbip
nropageonehudoe
eeyesyoushoulde
theplaceyouarek

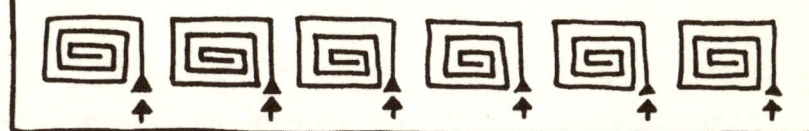

VOYAGE TO VICTORY

84

Room number eighty-four is the correct answer.

Finally they arrived in a room where all four doors were open. Lisa was punching the air like an insane boxer.

'This stupid little fly is really getting on my nerves!' she shouted.

Sam shook his head. 'Right, Brendan, which way?'

They looked around for a clue to which door they should take. The place however was empty.

'Perhaps I can help,' said a voice behind them.

They turned to face a tall, good-looking, blond-haired man. Where the heck did he come from? thought Sam.

'We're looking for a very special book,' said Brendan. 'It arrived here with Harold the Hairy Arm.'

'Well, I can't really help you,' the man said. 'You see, I don't live here. I'm just sort of visiting . . . as homeless gods do!'

He laughed to himself.

'You're a god!' gasped Lisa.

'One of them,' replied the man. 'It's Odin who lives here. He's the one who will be able to help you.'

'Where can we find him?' asked Sam.

'Oh, he's through one of those doors,' replied the man. 'But be sure to pick the correct one or you could spend eternity being lost in Valhalla.'

His lips formed a mischievous looking smile.

'Can you tell us which door to take . . . please?' asked Lisa politely.

'Sure!' replied the man. 'If you can tell me my name.'

He must be related to Rumpelstilskin, thought Lisa, glancing over at Sam.

Sam had turned his back to the man and was flicking through his museum booklet. He stopped on a page entitled 'Norse Gods'.

Opposite is a numbered list of some of the Norse gods. What is this god's name?
Turn to the same page as that number.

NORSE GODS

1. **ODIN** — Father of the gods, god of war, poetry and wisdom. He was powerful, treacherous and skilled in magic. He sacrificed one of his eyes to gain knowledge and understanding. He lived in Valhalla with his pet wolves, Geri and Freki, his eight-legged horse and his pet ravens who watched the world for him. Feared by both men and gods, his magic spear Grungir never missed its mark.

2. **THOR** — Son of Odin and god of thunder. He was a strong and fierce god who protected other gods and people from giants with the help of his hammer called Mjollnir (which means lightning). Vikings often wore hammer-shaped amulets around their necks to protect them. Thor rode in a chariot pulled by two giant goats. It was said that the sound of thunder was the clatter of these chariot wheels in the sky.

3. **FREYA** — The goddess of love and beauty. She rode in a chariot pulled by two great cats. Using her magic powers she could predict the future.

4. **FREY** — God of health, wealth, peace and nature. He made the sun shine, the rain fall and the crops grow. He was the twin brother of Freya and rode in a chariot pulled by a boar.

5. **FRIGG** — Frigg was the wife of Odin and looked after the health and wellbeing of people, especially children. She was kind and beautiful and had her own palace where she sat spinning thread into clouds.

6. **LOKI** — Part god, part demon. He was handsome and clever but also cunning and dishonest. He was a trickster whose practical jokes caused a lot of trouble for other gods. He was also a shapeshifter, which meant that he could turn himself into any animal or insect. Once when he was in the form of a mare he gave birth to an eight-legged horse.

7. **HEL** — Goddess of the dead. She was half dead and half alive. She was a very beautiful woman but from the waist down she was a hideous skeleton.

8. **HEIMDALL** — A gold-toothed god who guarded the Bifrost, the rainbow bridge connecting earth to Asgard (the land of the gods). His eyesight was so good that he could see in the dark. His hearing was so good that he could hear the wool growing on sheep. It was believed that he would blow his horn to announce the coming of Ragnarok (the end of the world).

9. **NJORD** — God of the sea and the winds. He protected those who travelled or went fishing. He had the most beautiful feet in the world which is why Skadi married him.

10. **SKADI** — The goddess of winter. Sometimes referred to as the 'Ice Queen'.

VOYAGE TO VICTORY
86

Person number eighty-six bought Lisa.

'I'm Knut,' said the Viking, cutting the ropes around Lisa's wrists and escorting her to a long wooden house with a thatched roof. A dead cow hung above the door! They were greeted by a woman wearing a funny-looking hat and a long dress with two large brooches on the front. Necklaces sparkled around her neck.

'I've got a present for you,' said the man, pointing to Lisa.

The woman smiled and took Lisa indoors.

'My name is Freyda,' she said. 'If you work hard for me you will be given a roof over your head and food for your belly. I am a fair woman. Now, follow me.'

She led Lisa up to the end of the house. In one corner there was a low bed lined with blankets and animal skins.

'This is where you will sleep,' informed Freyda. 'You will cook and clean. How's your weaving?' Freyda continued.

'Oh, fine,' replied Lisa. She didn't even know what weaving was. Something like knitting, wasn't it?

'Nice clothes!' said the woman, kneeling down to examine Lisa's jeans. 'But I don't like your shoes!'

Lisa was tempted to point out that they were called trainers, that they had cost her two months' pocket money and that they were very 'in' at the moment – well, not at this moment, but in her own 'time'. It was less complicated, however, to say nothing.

'Right,' said Freyda, handing Lisa a piece of silver jewellery. 'The first thing you can do is to find the comrade to this earring. It's somewhere in my jewellery box over there.'

Freyda nodded towards a box in the corner. The box was full of brooches, arm rings, necklaces, rings and earrings.

Glam lady! thought Lisa. She pulled out the earrings. They all looked identical.

Which one is the matching earring?
Turn to the same page as your answer.

FIND THE MATCH OF THIS EARRING

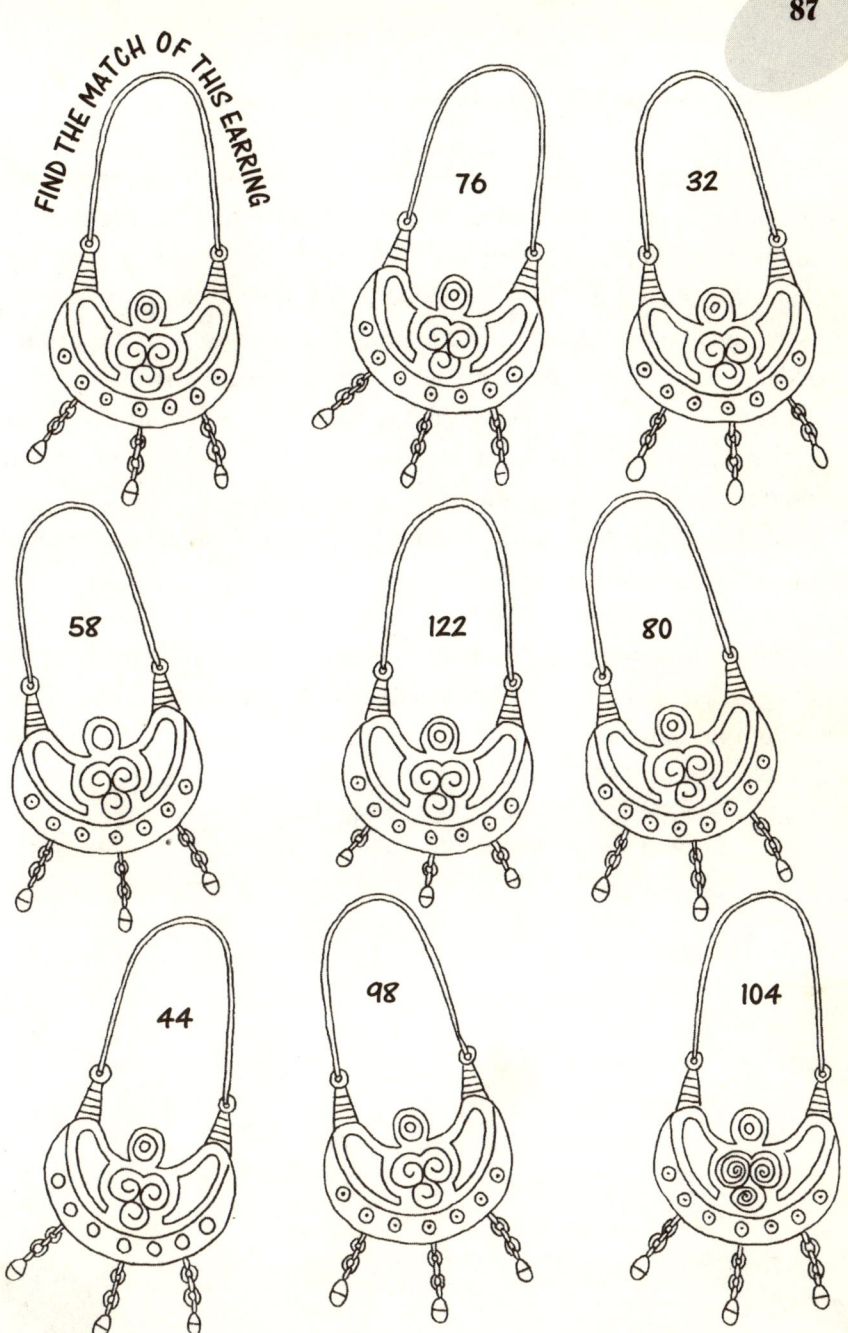

VOYAGE TO VICTORY
87

76 32

58 122 80

44 98 104

88

Door number eighty-eight is the correct answer.

Sam knew that once Miss Fussy had entered her lecturing mode, she wouldn't miss him. He had plenty of time to find Lisa and then go exploring. The place however was packed. People stood in wonder and awe as they inspected the many exhibits that littered the museum.

'Obviously some people have nothing better to do with their time,' pondered Sam, as he pushed his way through the crowds.

A few minutes later, having ducked and dived to avoid dangerous tourists, who walked blindly around absorbed in their maps and literature, Sam found himself at the Viking section.

A man in a suit put out his hand to stop Sam. A badge on his lapel indicated that he was museum staff.

Great! thought Sam. Caught already!

All the man was doing, however, was handing out booklets about the Vikings. He handed one to Sam and then looked away. Sam stuffed the booklet into the pocket of his rucksack and then surveyed the area for Lisa. No sign of her. He needed a better vantage point. Standing up on a nearby seat did just the trick. Now where was she?

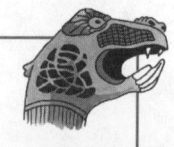

Can you find Lisa?
Turn to the same page as that number.

VOYAGE TO VICTORY
89

The door underneath the dead cow was slightly ajar. Sam and Brendan peeped in. Small metal and soapstone oil lamps were scattered around the room, creating enough light to see. The embers of a large fire glowed invitingly. The smell of food reminded the boys of how hungry they were. Asleep on the floor lay two large dogs. Through the tiny gap in the door, they could see the far end of the room and what they saw was a small sleeping figure curled up under some fur on the floor. Sam squinted his eyes to see more clearly. A pair of runners was sticking out from under the furs! He almost shouted with delight but then clasped his hand over his mouth, remembering the sleeping dogs. He backed away slowly from the door, beckoning to Brendan to follow him . . .

Inside, Lisa slept soundly. She was dreaming of a double bacon cheeseburger, fries and a large strawberry milkshake, but something was telling her to wake up. She tried to ignore this something because her dream was beautiful. In fact, it was more than beautiful, it was heavenly! She turned over but still something was telling her to wake up. What was it? A tapping noise, far away, but yet very close. She opened her eyes. The tapping was gentle but insistent. As well as taps, there were scrapes. She sat up in the bed. It was coming from the wall beside her. Somebody or something was scraping and tapping at the other side of the wall. It took her a few moments to realise what was going on. It was Morse code! She had used it earlier! Sam must be outside. There was silence and then the noises started again. Lisa began to decode the message. This is what she heard: tap, tap, scrape, tap . . . scrape, scrape, scrape . . . tap, scrape, tap, tap . . . tap, scrape, tap, tap . . . scrape, scrape, scrape . . . tap, scrape, scrape . . . scrape . . . tap, tap, tap, tap . . . tap . . . scrape, tap, tap . . . scrape, scrape, scrape . . . scrape, scrape, scrape . . . tap, scrape, tap.

VOYAGE TO VICTORY

91

Letter	Morse	Letter	Morse	Letter	Morse	Letter	Morse
A	.-	G	--.	N	-.	U	..-
B	-...	H	....	O	---	V	...-
C	-.-.	I	..	P	.--.	W	.--
D	-..	J	.---	Q	--.-	X	-..-
E	.	K	-.-	R	.-.	Y	-.--
F	..-.	L	.-..	S	...	Z	--..
		M	--	T	-		

A scrape is a dash (–) and a tap is a dot (.)
What is Sam's message?
Turn to the same page as the symbol in his message.

Sword piece number ninety-two is the correct answer.

Olaf appeared at the door of the forge. 'Right you two, let's go!'

He escorted Sam and Brendan around the outskirts of the town to a grassy area full of tents. Horses were tied up in small groups. There were women cooking food on fires and people chatting to each other, but mostly, people were buying or selling various goods which were laid out neatly on coloured cloth.

'There are traders here from all over the world,' explained Olaf.

You could tell who the foreigners were because they dressed differently. They wore fur-trimmed hats and baggy trousers which were bound tightly around the lower leg.

'Trendy!' smirked Sam.

'I need you to help me,' whispered Olaf to the children. 'You see, I'm not as quick as I used to be and I don't want any merchant pulling a fast one on me. Will you make sure that I don't pay too much?'

He approached an Arab trader who was selling coloured silk.

'How much?' enquired Olaf.

'Two and a half coins an ell,' said the trader.

Sam and Brendan were determined to do as Olaf had requested.

'What's an ell?' asked Brendan.

'The distance between my elbow and my fingertips,' replied the merchant.

'It's a pity your arms aren't a bit longer then!' mumbled Sam.

Luckily the merchant didn't hear him.

'And how can you have half a coin?' asked Sam.

The merchant's patience was growing thin. He whipped a silver coin out of Olaf's hand and snapped it in half. He then handed the two halves back, smiling cheekily at Sam.

'All right then,' said Olaf. 'I'll have sixteen ells of red silk.'

VOYAGE TO VICTORY
93

How many coins should Olaf pay the trader?
Turn to the same page as your answer.

The sun symbol is part of Lisa's message.

Sam was glad that Lisa was OK. He sat down in the darkness. Neither himself nor Brendan felt like talking. They were both too worried about what would happen to them next. An hour later the door was reopened and Scarface pulled the children out. Sam was happy to see Lisa again. The prisoners were taken along to a grassy area of the town. A large crowd had gathered around a wooden stage where a group of dejected men stood with their hands tied. Brendan recognised the men from his monastery back home. They used to be his neighbours.

The three children were put up on the wooden platform with the rest of the prisoners. The crowd fell silent, as if there was going to be an execution. Luckily, this was not the case. The children watched in awe as one by one, the men were brought to the front of the stage to be sold! Different Vikings raised their hands in competition with each other as they bid for each prisoner. When a sale was made, the buyer paid Scarface a sum of silver and then took his purchase away. Soon there was nobody left on the stage except for the children. Sam and Brendan were bundled together in one corner of the stage, with Lisa on the other. Lisa gave her friends a puzzled look.

'Two for the price of one!' whispered Sam.

Lisa smiled and then faced the bidders. A bald man raised his hand to bid. The man to his left quickly put in another bid. A third bid came from a man with one eye. The first man bid again, then the third man and then the second man. There were no more bids.

It was now Sam and Brendan's turn. A fierce-looking man with a helmet made the first bid. His bid was followed by a man wearing a cap then another Viking to his right put in a bid. He was unchallenged.

The children, scared and worried, were led away by their new owners.

VOYAGE TO VICTORY
95

To follow Lisa, turn to the same page as the number on the person who bought her.
Follow Sam and Brendan by turning to the same page as the number on the person who bought them.
When you have followed both groups, turn to page 90.

VOYAGE TO VICTORY

96

***Book of Time* page ninety-six is the correct answer.**

The page was in code. Three brains raced to crack it.

VOYAGE TO VICTORY

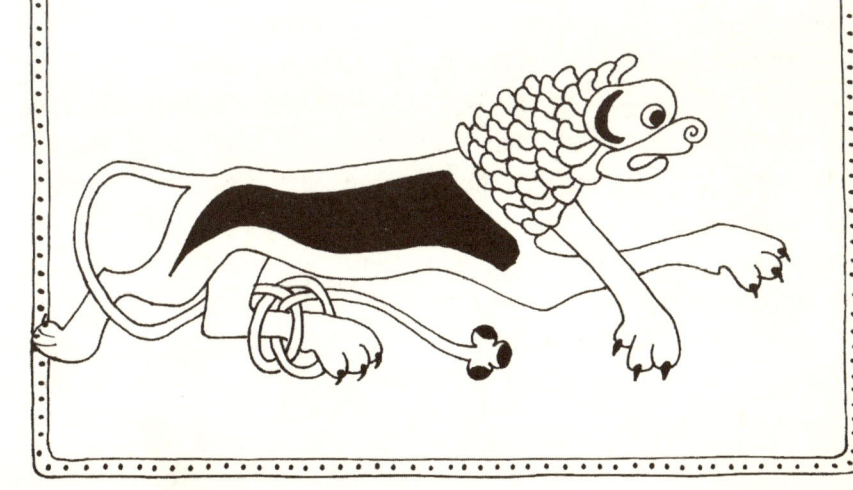

97

ecalp na tcejbo no
eht koob. eht tcejbo
tsum emoc morf
eht ecalp dna emit
ot hcihw uoy hsiw
ot nruter. nrut ot
egap ytneves owt.

98

Earring number ninety-eight is the correct answer.

'Next thing I want you to do,' ordered Freyda, 'is to go into town. There you will see a building with a cart full of boxes outside. Inside a man called Eirik will give you a box of gifts that my brother brought home for me. There should be a book, a necklace, a candlestick and a golden cup in it. Tell Eirik that I sent you.'

Lisa was glad to leave the house and get some fresh air. The town was full of wooden houses with thatched roofs. The streets were paved with wooden planks. Fish were being dried on wooden sticks for storage. Some of the houses had animals in their backyards. The place was full of activity. Men were feeding animals, chopping wood or carrying goods up and down the street. A stream flowed through the middle of the town and in it a group of women were washing their clothes. Lisa giggled to herself when she came across a group of naked boys having a bath in the same stream. A little further on, she was disgusted, however, to find a woman dumping her rubbish in the water. Lisa stood up on a discarded barrel to see further. In the distance, at the edge of the town, she could see a grassy area full of tents.

Must be a holiday resort, laughed Lisa to herself. I wonder where the slot machines and the ice-cream vans are!

Smiling, she continued on her journey. She passed shoemakers, comb-makers, people selling clay pots and women chatting or drawing water from a well. Eventually, she spotted the building with the cart outside. Upon entering she was greeted by a man (presumably Eirik).

'Freyda sent me,' smiled Lisa.

'Oh, r-right,' stuttered Eirik. 'Now, I wonder which box is h-hers.'

Which number box is Freyda's?
Turn to the same page as your answer.

VOYAGE TO VICTORY
99

The Valhalla symbol is the correct answer.

The children headed in the direction of Valhalla.

'I wonder where I would go if I stepped off this road,' pondered Sam, peering over the edge of the road and into the blackness.

It was a strange sort of blackness. It wasn't solid, yet you couldn't see through it or into it.

'Rather you than me!' smiled Lisa.

As they walked, something began to materialise in the distance although they couldn't tell what it was. The further they walked, however, the larger it grew, rising up in front of them.

'Well at least we know that we're making progress,' said Brendan. 'Whatever it is, it's getting closer.'

It turned out to be a gigantic building . . . a palace of some sort.

'Valhalla!' gasped Sam. 'Hall of the Slain!'

The ground stretched out on either side of the road ahead of them to accommodate this colossal structure. The children had never seen anything so big. It was rectangular in shape, with thousands of narrow windows. A dome-shaped roof towered up into the clouds. Steps led up to a large wooden door and above it an eagle sat perched watching the children's every move.

'Well,' shrugged Sam. 'Only one way to go!'

The children climbed the stone steps. On the door was a sign carved in runes.

'Get out that booklet again, Sam!' ordered Lisa.

'What would you do without me?' he smiled.

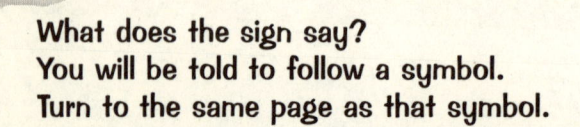

What does the sign say?
You will be told to follow a symbol.
Turn to the same page as that symbol.

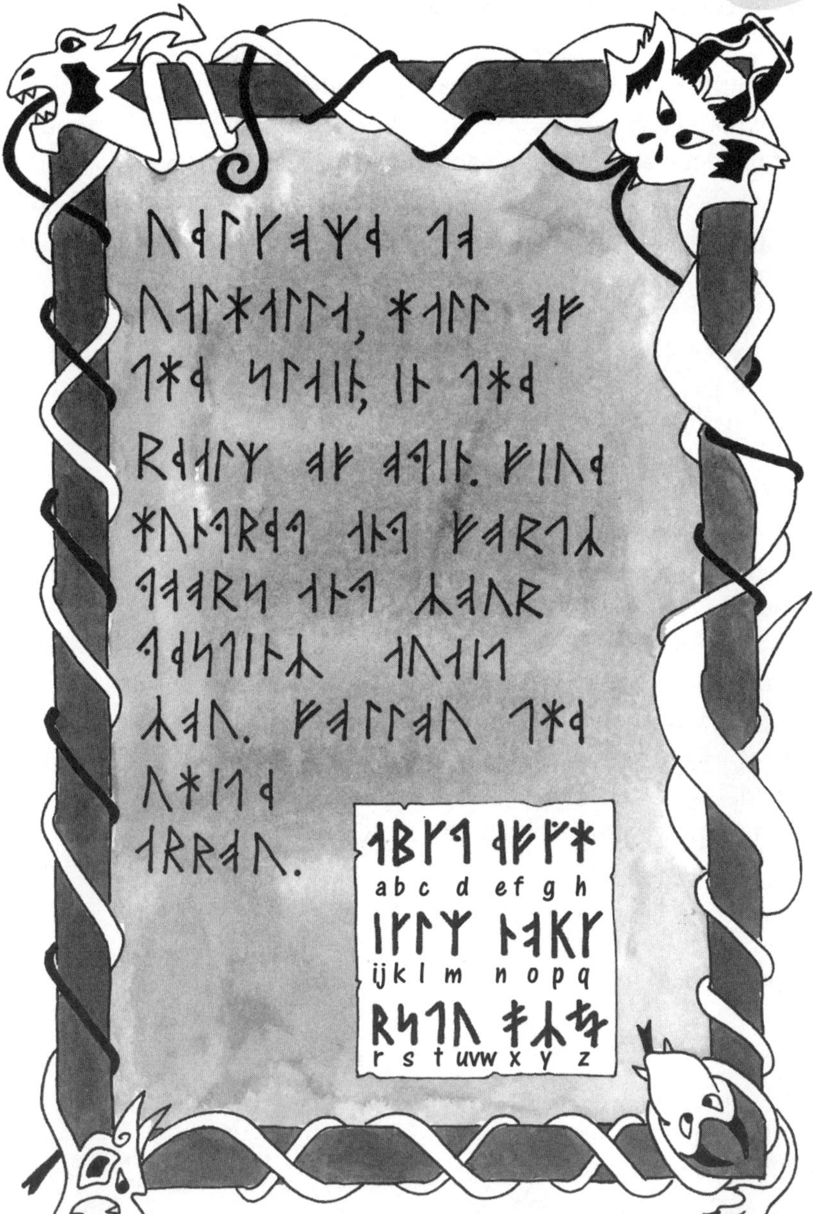
a b c d e f g h
ij k l m n o p q
r s t uvw x y z

VOYAGE TO VICTORY
102

The bird symbol is the correct answer.

A few birds had landed on the deck to eat the grain that Sam had spilled during the night.

'If there are birds,' exclaimed Lisa, 'then there must be land nearby!'

Soon the children glimpsed their first sight of land. The Vikings gave a cheer and kissed a hammer-shaped pendant around their necks.

'Thank Thor!' shouted one of the men.

The sail was let down and the Vikings rowed the ship towards land. As the ship got closer to the shore, the children could distinguish a small town. A large crowd waited on the shore. They cheered and waved swords as the ship approached. All of a sudden, Scarface and a burly mate grabbed the three children and tied their hands behind their backs. They were then connected to a long rope.

'Here we go again,' moaned Lisa.

Men, women and children waded out into the shallow water to help unload the goods. The children were lifted into the water and led ashore by Scarface. He brought them up into the town, which consisted of small houses with thatched roofs. Stopping at a small stone building with two wooden doors, he cut Sam and Brendan free and shoved them into one room, pushing Lisa into the other. Sam banged at the door and shouted, but it was no use. They were locked in.

'I hope Lisa's OK,' he whimpered, slumping down onto the floor.

All of a sudden, the sound of scraping and tapping could be heard at the other side of the wall. It wasn't just any old scraping and tapping – it was Morse code!

Out of boredom last summer, Sam and Lisa had learned the Morse code off by heart. Lisa must be trying to contact him, but what was she saying? This is what Sam heard: tap, tap. . . tap, scrape . . . scrape, scrape . . . scrape, scrape, scrape . . . scrape, tap, scrape, . . . tap, tap, scrape, tap . . . scrape, scrape, scrape . . . tap, scrape, tap, tap . . . tap, scrape, tap, tap . . . scrape, scrape, scrape . . . tap, scrape, scrape . . . scrape . . . tap, tap, tap, tap, . . . tap . . . tap, tap, tap . . . tap, tap, scrape . . . scrape, tap.

VOYAGE TO VICTORY
103

Letter	Morse	Letter	Morse	Letter	Morse	Letter	Morse
A	.-	G	--.	N	-.	U	..-
B	-...	H	....	O	---	V	...-
C	-.-.	I	..	P	.--.	W	.--
D	-..	J	.---	Q	--.-	X	-..-
E	.	K	-.-	R	.-.	Y	-.--
F	..-.	L	.-..	S	...	Z	--..
		M	--	T	-		

A scrape is a dash(-) and a tap is a dot(.).
Translate the scrapes and taps into
Morse code to find out what Lisa is saying.
Turn to the same page as the symbol in her message.

The comb is the correct symbol.

'Everything except combs,' said Lisa, returning the list to Knucklehead.

'Ha!' he laughed. 'With no ladies, we can afford to be scruffy!'

He grabbed Lisa in one hand and Sam in the other and marched them down to the middle of the ship. Among the provisions was a small crate lined with animal skins.

'This will be your home for the next few weeks,' snarled Knucklehead, pushing the children into the crate. 'Step out of here and the three of you will feel the cold steel of my blade on your throats!'

He lifted a crude-looking dagger from his belt, licked it with his tongue, laughed and then walked off.

'Big gorilla's backside!' muttered Sam.

'Why did he say the three of us?' asked Lisa.

The answer to this question came in the form of movement from under one of the animal skins. A little head emerged. It was the boy from the round tower! His big brown eyes were full of tears but he smiled when he saw Sam and Lisa.

'They took my crucifix and my rosary beads,' he snivelled.

'Don't worry,' said Lisa, putting her hand on the boy's shoulder. 'We'll get them back for you. Now, who has them?'

'A man called Scarface. He's taking stuff from everyone,' the boy whimpered, pointing to the top of the ship.

Sure enough, a large Viking with a scar on his cheek was taking jewellery from one of the captives. He began to walk towards the children.

Sam emptied out the contents of his rucksack, most of which were luckily still dry. He put all his own stuff into Lisa's rucksack, which already contained a walkie-talkie, lunch box, copy and pencil. He then shoved the bag towards Lisa.

'Quick!' he said. 'Hide it under those animal skins!'

VOYAGE TO VICTORY
105

How many objects are now in Lisa's rucksack?
Turn to the same page as your answer.

One hundred and six is the correct answer.

Lisa was first to open her eyes. She was petrified to look around her. She squeezed her friends' hands, causing them to open their eyes. Brendan looked around. It took him a few seconds to recognise the interior of the small church in his monastery.

'I'm home! I'm home!' he shouted, jumping up and down with excitement.

He raced out the door. The sight of the countryside outside told Sam and Lisa that *they* weren't home.

'All right for you,' said Lisa. 'But what about us?'

Sam and Lisa followed Brendan out the door but by the time they stepped outside something strange had happened. The place was full of people. They wore jeans and tracksuits and runners and leather jackets! They had glasses, mobile phones and prams!

'We're back in the museum,' gibbered Sam, stunned at this realisation.

Lisa was never so glad to see imitation grass, imitation stone churches, information signs, dustbins and security guards.

'Déjà vu or what!' marvelled Lisa.

'Déjà what?' frowned Sam.

'Forget it,' smiled Lisa. 'We're home!'

'They you are!' scorned a voice from not too far away.

It was Miss Fussy. Sam couldn't believe that he actually felt happy to see his teacher again.

'You two were supposed to be back from lunch at 1.30. It's now 2.46,' scolded Miss Fussy, checking her watch. 'Do you realise how many minutes late you are?'

She raised her eyebrows and waited for an answer.

You can't be serious, thought Sam.

But Miss Fussy was serious – deadly serious.

VOYAGE TO VICTORY
107

How many minutes late are the children?
Turn to the same page as your answer.

VOYAGE TO VICTORY 108

Sack number one hundred and eight is the correct answer.

The children just managed to grab the sack and make it out of the storeroom before Eirik returned. They watched him lock the door and vanish into the darkness of the night.

'Do you really think that the *Book of Time* can take us home?' Brendan asked Lisa. His voice seemed to lack enthusiasm.

'I don't know,' shrugged Lisa. 'But it's the only thing that we have to link our time with this time. Sam and I believe it's the reason that we're here. In fact, it's the reason that you're here as well.'

'Let's go!' urged Sam. 'We shouldn't be wasting time talking.'

Lisa raised her eyebrows. Brendan sensed an argument and interrupted. 'Presuming that Harold has the book how do we find out where he lives?'

The only answer he received was silence. Sam had switched on his torch and was flashing it around. The torch revealed a stone set in the ground. Strange symbols were carved on the stone.

'They're runes,' informed Lisa, remembering her history lessons. 'Vikings used them instead of letters.'

'Can you read what it says?' asked Brendan.

Lisa shook her head. Sam began rummaging through the rucksack. He took out the booklet that he had been given in the museum. Smiling, he began to read from the book.

'The alphabet is called Futhark and is formed mainly by straight lines to make it easy to carve the runes onto wood or stone. Stones have been found in Viking towns detailing heroic deeds by Viking warriors. And this,' continued Sam, holding open the page, 'tells you what letter each rune represents.'

'Well done,' said Brendan. 'Perhaps there's a clue on this stone.'

VOYAGE TO VICTORY
109

a b c d e f g h
i j k l m n o p q
r s t u v w x y z

Translate the runes into letters.
You will be told to follow a symbol.
Turn to the same page as that symbol.

Door number one hundred and ten is the correct answer.

The children pushed open the old door and left the maze behind them. They now found themselves in a stable of some sort. A large grey horse stared at the children. It was a rather ordinary animal in most respects except one. It had eight legs! A disgusting stench reached the children's nostrils. Glancing around, they saw piles of horse dung heaped up in one corner. As in the other room, the ceiling was made up of shields and spears. The far wall was lined with wooden doors. Each door was marked with a different symbol.

'This is not getting any easier,' Lisa grumbled to the boys.

The horse snorted and somehow managed to roll back its upper and lower lips, revealing a large set of yellowed teeth. What was even more bizarre was the fact that seven of its teeth were marked with different symbols. It was as if someone had painted them on with black paint.

'They're runes,' revealed Brendan. 'Quick, translate!'

Sam found the appropriate page of his now invaluable booklet and began to call out the letters as he translated them.

'W-E-L-C-O-M-E,' he said.

'Wow!' marvelled Lisa. 'What an amazing creature. I wonder what its name is?'

The horse closed its lips, snorted and then exposed its teeth again but this time they bore different runes.

'S-L-E-I-P-N-I-R,' called out Sam as he studied his booklet.

'Perhaps, Sleipnir, you can help us,' said Brendan to the horse. 'You see, we're looking for a book, the *Book of Time*, to be exact.'

The horse snorted and shook its head.

'What about Odin?' questioned Lisa. 'Do you know where we can find him?'

The horse snorted and once again exposed its teeth with a new set of runes.

VOYAGE TO VICTORY

111

```
abcd efgh
ijkl m nopq
rstuvw xyz
```

Quick, translate!
Turn to the same page as that symbol.

Building number one hundred and twelve is the correct answer.

The monk's head popped out of one of the narrow windows of the round tower.

'Hurry up, you two!' he hissed, throwing down a rope ladder.

Delighted to have company again, Lisa began climbing the ladder. Sam was hesitant. He could hear something in the distance. It sounded like a crowd roaring, a battle cry of some sort. Quickly, he scrambled up the ladder. The monk pushed the two children down wooden steps into the base of the tower and then reeled in the ladder. Inside the tower was dark and very cramped. A man, a woman, a boy and two monks stood with their backs to the stone wall. Each held a small candle which created a circle of light and illuminated the objects in the middle of the floor. Golden chalices, candlesticks and crosses sparkled in the candlelight. Lisa recognised some of the golden objects that they had collected in the museum. There were also piles of large, heavy and very ornate-looking books stacked on the earthen floor.

The four adults looked extremely worried and were so busy whispering to each other that they didn't even notice Sam and Lisa enter. Higher up in the tower, the two friends could hear people running up and down steps and the banging of wooden boards.

'They're blocking the tower windows,' whispered a voice beside them. It was the young boy. He hadn't taken his eyes off Sam and Lisa since they had stumbled down the steps and had made his way over to them. His hair was long, his clothes were shabby.

'But why?' enquired Sam.

'We have to protect the valuables from the raiders and especially the *Book of Time*,' whispered the boy, pointing to the pile of books on the floor.

'Which book is it?' asked Lisa, squinting her eyes to see.

'The one with the diamonds, circles, triangles and squares.'

VOYAGE TO VICTORY
113

Which number book is the <u>Book of Time</u>?
Turn to the same page as your answer.

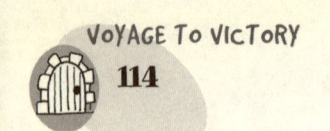

The door symbol is the correct answer.

Lisa tiptoed towards the door. The dogs didn't stir and Freyda and her husband were sleeping at the other end of the house. She pulled the door gently but it creaked as if in pain. Lisa froze. There was movement behind her. She turned to see one of the dogs watching her. When the dog saw her face, he closed his eyes again. She pulled the door open just enough to slip out. Upon seeing Sam and Brendan, she raced over and gave each of them a big hug.

'Watch the threads!' scorned an embarrassed Sam, unruffling his jumper. Secretly, he was delighted to see her.

The three children spent the next few minutes in whispers, telling each other of their day's events. Lisa informed the boys of what she had heard about Harold the Hairy Arm.

'OK!' whispered Sam. 'Let's not waste any more time. If he dies, we may never find the *Book of Time*!'

They set off walking but found it difficult to see properly.

'If only I had my torch!' whispered Sam.

There was silence for a moment and then Lisa said, 'I think I might just know where our gear is. Follow me.'

She cautiously led the way through the town. When she saw the outline of the cart, she knew that she had found the storeroom. The door was open and a yellow light flickered inside. A shadow darted across the floor. Someone was there. Lisa peeped in. It was Eirik and he was searching for something.

'Damn keys!' he mumbled. 'I must have left them at home.'

'Quick!' urged Lisa. 'Hide!'

The three children dived behind the old cart and watched Eirik leave the storeroom and disappear up the street.

'Right,' whispered Lisa, running inside. 'We haven't got much time.'

VOYAGE TO VICTORY
115

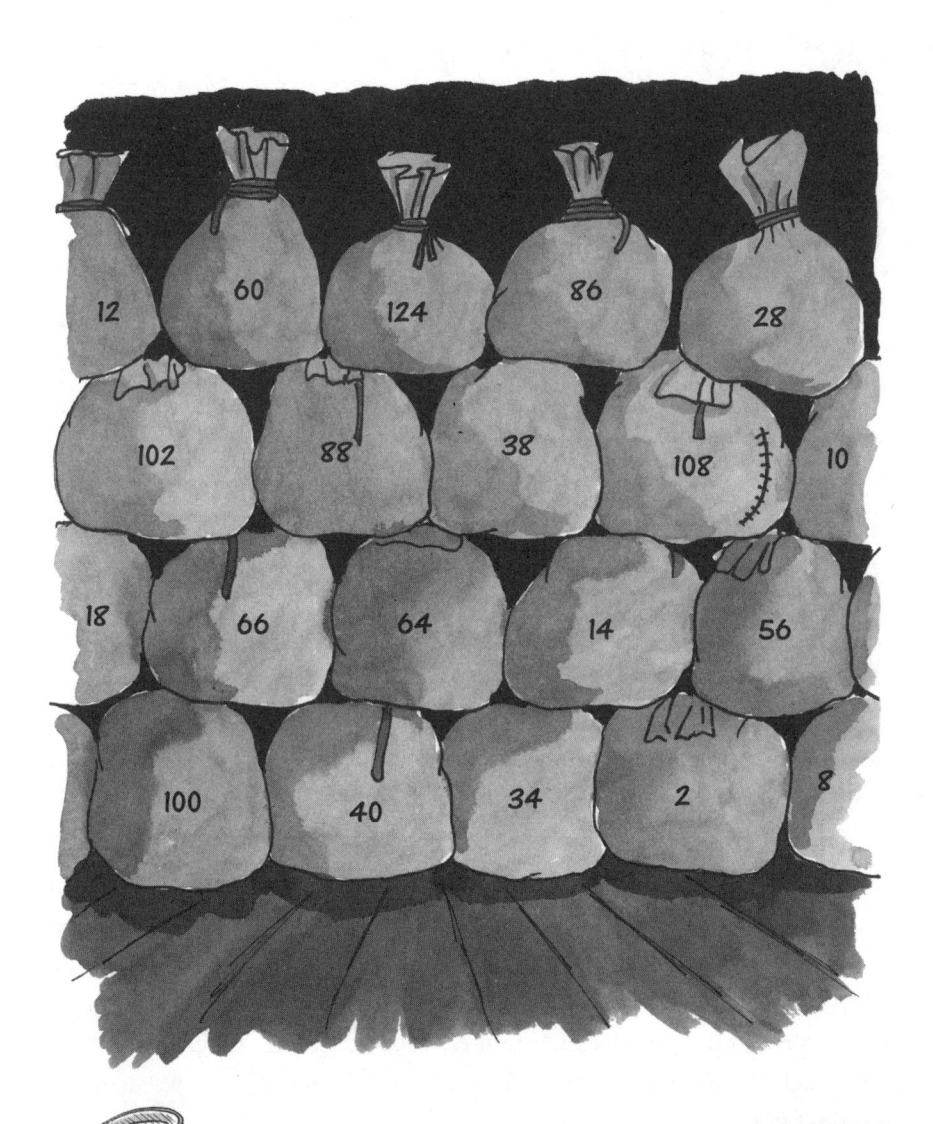

In which sack is the rucksack hidden?
Turn to the same page as that number.

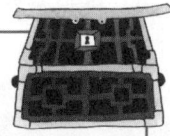

The fish symbol is the correct answer.

The children had been in danger before, but this time there was no escape. They would either drown or be burnt alive. Meanwhile, the ship continued to smash through the waves. It seemed to be picking up speed, being driven by an invisible force, destined for some unknown place. A sharp wind streamed past the children's faces, causing the flames to flicker nervously. Sam frowned in disbelief.

'What the heck is going on?' he thought to himself.

The ship was now speeding across the dark sea. For balance, the children grabbed the mast. Lisa raised her face to the sky. A gentle mist was falling. This soon turned into rain. One by one, the flames died down until all that was left were the glowing cinders of burnt wood. The children watched in amazement as these orange cinders were slowly dissolved by the rain into a dull grey and then black. The ship was now engulfed in the pitch blackness of night. The three voyagers were all too stunned to speak. They held onto the mast for dear life as the ship raced across the ocean.

Had this been an ordinary night, the children wouldn't have believed their eyes when a rainbow appeared in the sky, but then again, this was no ordinary night. The rainbow was luminous in its multitude of colours, as if someone had painted it onto the black canvas of night. Normally, a rainbow doesn't get closer as you travel towards it, which is why crocks of gold are never found, but a night rainbow is different. The arc of colour seemed to be almost solid, with both ends planted firmly in the sea. The ship was heading for one end of the rainbow and the closer they got, the larger and brighter the rainbow got. Soon the ship was drenched in red, orange, yellow, green, blue, indigo and violet. The rainbow towered above the children like a waterfall of colours coming from the sky.

VOYAGE TO VICTORY
117

How many colours are in the rainbow?
Multiply this by 4 and then add 14.
Turn to the same page as your answer.

***Book of Time* page one hundred and eighteen is the correct answer.**

'OK!' chirped Lisa. 'Let's do it.'

Brendan placed his rosary beads on the book. From the rucksack Sam removed his magnifying glass and Lisa's pencil. He placed these alongside the beads.

'Now, something from this place and time,' said Sam, surveying the contents of the room.

'How about this?' said Brendan, dragging over a large battle-axe. The axe was placed under the book.

Next, the children stood around the book, each making sure that their feet touched it.

'Now hold hands,' urged Lisa.

Hands were locked, so that a circle of hands hovered above the book.

'Right, on the count of three, let's say the magic words and don't forget,' reminded Lisa, 'to keep your eyes closed and imagine the place where you are going. One . . . two . . . '

'Wait!' shouted Sam. 'What are the words again?'

Lisa sighed.

'*Book of Time, Book of Time.* Return me to the place that is M . . . I . . . N . . . E,' she said.

'Why didn't you say the word "mine"?' enquired Brendan.

'Just in case the spell worked and I was transported home on my own!' she replied.

'Good thinking!' he said.

'Now, have you got all that, Sam?' asked Lisa, a slight hint of mockery in her voice.

'Yeah, yeah, let's get on with it!' he retorted.

'One . . . two . . . three!' counted Lisa.

'*Book of Time, Book of Time.* Return me to the place that is mine.'

VOYAGE TO VICTORY
119

Multiply the number of objects on the <u>Book of Time</u> by 35 and add 1.
Turn to the same page as your answer.

VOYAGE TO VICTORY

A 120

Book of Time page one hundred and twenty is the correct answer.

'I hope you're remembering all this,' said Sam to Lisa.

'Of course!' was Lisa's reply.

VOYAGE TO VICTORY

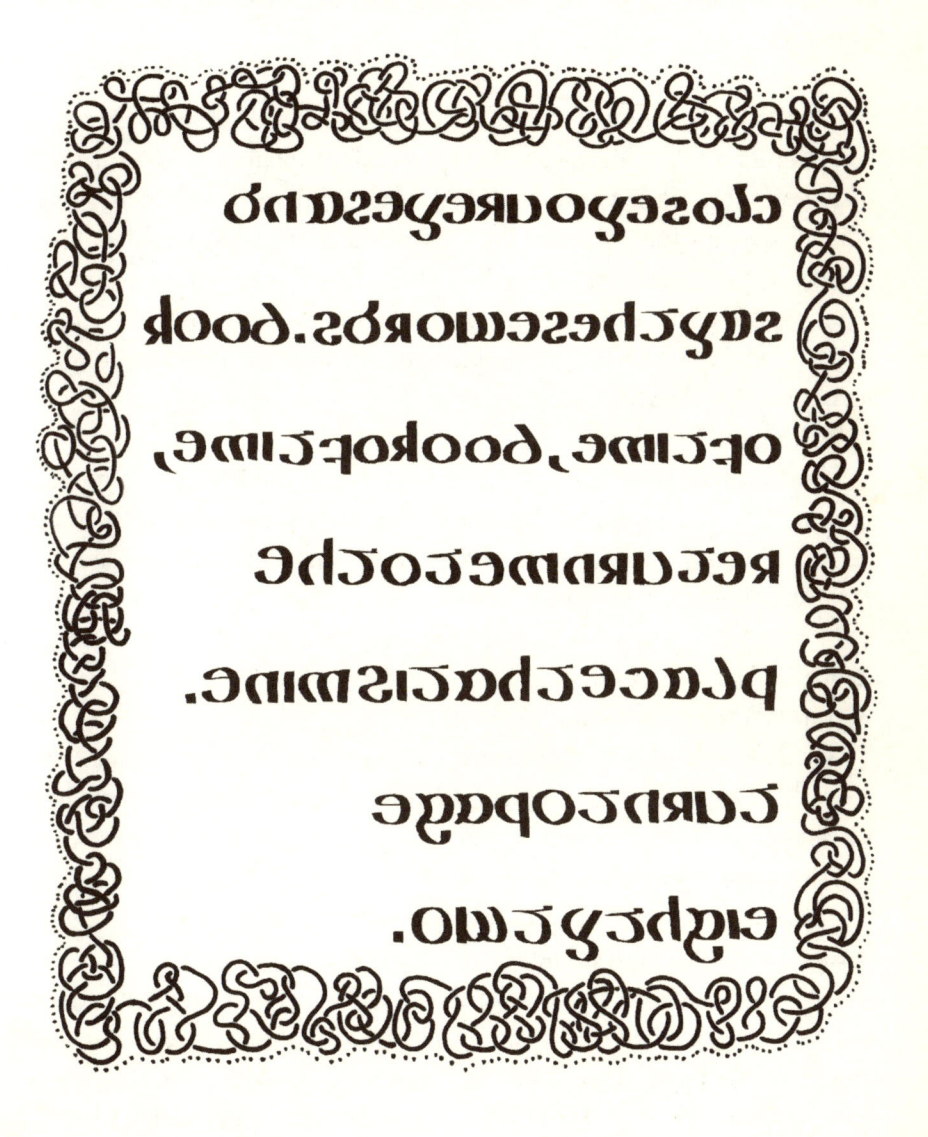

121

> close your eyes and
> say these words. look
> of time, book of time,
> recap me to the
> place that is mine.
> turn to page
> eighty two.

Person number one hundred and twenty-two is the correct answer.

As they travelled along in the cart, they could see nothing, but the sound of the sea got louder and louder. A soft crunching noise indicated that they were on a beach. Suddenly the children found themselves being lifted up into the air. They could hear mumbling and talking under the cart. They rocked backwards and forwards and after a lot of banging, shouting and struggling, the cart seemed to be returned to solid ground – or so they thought. It didn't take the children long to recognise that familiar feeling you get when you're on the sea.

'Not again!' thought Lisa.

There seemed to be a lot of movement all around but Sam, Brendan or Lisa didn't make a sound. If they were discovered now, they could be in big trouble. All of a sudden a crackling sound surrounded the children. It was a familiar sound but they couldn't think what it could be. It was only when black smoke invaded the cart that the children realised what was going on.

'Fire!' whimpered Sam.

Brendan looked out. They were on a ship loaded with objects and everything was on fire! Small lights in the distance meant that they were already a long way from the shore. The ship was now moving rapidly, crashing through the black waves, even though it had no sail. The children looked around. There was nobody else on board, nobody, that is, except for Harold the Hairy Arm and he was already dead! The flames danced higher, licking the sides of the boat and surrounding the children with a terrifying blaze. They huddled together close to the centre of the ship. Lisa and Sam were numb with fear. Brendan, however, seemed calm. He knelt down on the deck, removed his rosary beads from around his neck and began to pray.

VOYAGE TO VICTORY

123

Find the symbol in the picture.
Turn to the page with that symbol.

One hundred and twenty-four is the correct answer.

Mr Snore began to speak again. 'This hasn't been the first time the book has survived a robbery. Over the centuries, many attempts have been made to steal the book, but somehow it has always remained safe. There is one story in the book, written in the year 828 by the monks of Briar Hill Monastery, that tells the tale of Viking raiders stealing the book and taking it back to Norway. The story tells of how the book was nearly burned on a ship with the body of a heroic Viking called Harold the Hairy Arm. According to the story, a local boy from the monastery, who was taken as a slave by the same Viking raiders, rescued the book with the help of two mysterious children. In the story the two children are referred to as "wonder children", because of their strange looks and unusual ways. The children are believed to have been time travellers from the future!'

Lisa's mouth dropped open.

'The *Book of Time*, however, is full of strange legends like this one,' continued Mr Snore, 'and legends, as you know, are not always true, but fun all the same!'

Sam and Lisa daydreamed through the rest of the school tour, oblivious to everything else that went on. They were both trying to work out everything that had happened. They thought of Brendan, who had been their friend for so long, even though it now seemed that they had only been away for minutes. They would miss him, but they knew that he was in a happy place, just as they were happy to be home.

Sam and Lisa looked forward to seeing their parents again and, somewhere in the back of their minds, they looked forward to the approaching summer holidays. Who knows what adventures they would bring!

VOYAGE TO VICTORY

Page	Answer	Page	Answer	Page	Answer	Page	Answer
2-3	28	34-35	96	64-65	14	94-95	86/44
4-5	66	36-37	62	66-67	12	96-97	72
6-7	110	38-39	95	68-69	122	98-99	54
8-9	92	40-41	56	70-71	34	100-101	60
10-11	50	42-43	22	72-73	16	102-103	94
12-13	46	44-45	8	74-75	36	104-105	20
14-15	32	46-47	80	76-77	124	106-107	76
16-17	78	48-49	88	78-79	120	108-109	68
18-19	102	50-51	84	80-81	64	110-111	30
20-21	4	52-53	58	82-83	118	112-113	74
22-23	100	54-55	38	84-85	6	114-115	108
24-25	70	56-57	95	86-87	98	116-117	42
26-27	112	58-59	26	88-89	52	118-119	106
28-29	48	60-61	10	90-91	114	120-121	82
30-31	24	62-63	104	92-93	40	122-123	116
32-33	18						

Also from Kieran Fanning

Trapdoor to Treachery

Sam and Lisa decide to do some investigating when a series of mysterious thefts plagues their town. Following the trail of the thief, they are led into a strange and exciting world full of puzzles, elves and gobbledegooks. They must take care, however, as danger lurks around every corner.

You must help Sam and Lisa search for clues, crack codes and solve many other tricky puzzles in their quest to catch the master criminal.